VOID
Library of
Davidson College

*"Variations Without a Theme"
and Other Stories
by
Xu Xing*

Published by Wild Peony Pty Ltd ACN 002 714 276
PO Box 636 Broadway NSW 2007 Australia
Fax 61 2 9566 1052

International Distribution:
University of Hawaii Press
2480 Kolowalu Street
Honolulu, Hawaii 96822, USA

Copyright © Wild Peony Pty Ltd.

First published 1997

All rights reserved. No part of this publication may be reproduced, stored in a retrieval system or transmitted in any form or by any means electronic, mechanical, photocopying, recording or otherwise without the prior permission of the publisher.

ISBN 0 9586526 2 7

Printed in Australia by National Capital Printing, Canberra

"Variations Without a Theme" and Other Stories by Xu Xing

Translated with Introduction by

Maria Galikowski
&
Lin Min

UNIVERSITY OF SYDNEY EAST ASIAN SERIES NUMBER 11

WILD PEONY

For the publication of this volume we acknowledge
the generous support of

The Department of East Asian Studies,
University of Waikato, New Zealand

The four stories by Xu Xing in this volume have been translated
from Xu Xing, *Wu zhuti bianzou*
(Zuojia chubanshe, Beijing, 1989).

CONTENTS

Fragmentation and Heterogeneity: Xu Xing's Literary
    Treatment of the Contemporary Human Condition   1

On a Side Road   25

Martyr   40

Variations Without a Theme   49

Story of a City   81

Fragmentation and Heterogeneity: Xu Xing's Literary Treatment of the Contemporary Human Condition

The short stories of Xu Xing, together with Liu Suola's "You Have No Choice", are considered by many to be the first modernist pieces in contemporary Chinese literature, providing the impetus for China's literary trend of modernism during the 1980s[1]. Xu Xing was born in 1956 in Beijing. His father was an engineer in the Ministry of Forestry and his mother worked as a hospital gynaecologist. Like many thousands of intellectuals, his father was treated harshly during the Anti-Rightist Movement (1957) and the Cultural Revolution (1966–76). When Xu Xing was only eleven years old, his mother went to far-off Gansu province in response to official calls

---

[1] See Chen Xiaoming, "Zui houde yishi" in *Wenxue pinglun*, 5 (1991), pp. 128–29. The modernists sent shock waves throughout the Chinese literary scene with their unprecedented challenge of conventional literary norms. One Chinese critic commented on their impact: "Life no longer has only one explanation, and the arts also are no longer limited to only a few fixed modes of expression." See Lei Da, "Zhuti yishi de qianghua" in *Renmin wenxue*, 1 (1986), p. 123. It should be noted that, in the context of cultural development in contemporary China, the notions of modernism and post-modernism are very much interwoven. The rapidity with which the avant-garde literary and artistic movement gained momentum in post-Mao China meant that these two phases of cultural development quickly merged to become a major creative force, particularly among the younger generation of writers and artists. It would be appropriate to say that the writings of Xu Xing and others exhibit a certain continuity between the pre-modern, the modern and the post-modern, an experimental synthesis which defies definition based on rigid and narrow systems of classification.

for intellectuals to re-educate themselves through labour. With his older siblings having been sent to work in the countryside, he was forced to fend for himself. Over the next few years, he wandered aimlessly around China, encountering many different kinds of people and situations. By 1975 he had finished high school and, after two years living and working with peasants in Yan'an, Shaanxi province, he joined the army. In 1981 he returned to Beijing and was assigned a job in a Peking-duck restaurant, where he worked at various times as a waiter and a cleaner. His frequent failure to turn up for work and lack of punctuality, however, resulted in his subsequent dismissal. He remained unemployed until 1987 when he secured temporary work at the Lu Xun Academy of Art, and also as editor of the journal *Huaren shijie* (Chinese World). Since the early 1980s several of his short stories have been published in major literary journals, including *Renmin wenxue* (The People's Literature). In November 1989 he visited Germany at the invitation of the West Berlin Academy of Arts, and while there he participated in the re-launch of the literary journal *Jintian* (Today). He returned to China in 1993 and continues to live in Beijing.

From the time Xu Xing first came to prominence, he was clearly of a different mould from that of the older generation of Chinese writers, many of whom tended to see their role not only as the creators of literature, but also as ideological spokespeople and authoritative arbiters of social and moral values. Xu Xing by contrast, does not moralize, and his work does not convey an overt political message, though at the same time it is neither ideologically neutral nor devoid of social criticism. A product of the momentous transformations that have taken place in contemporary Chinese society, it offers an insightful reflection of the mood and psychological state of individuals during a period of rapid social transition. What his stories convey above all is a deep and complex sense of ontological dislocation, the manifestation of a spiritual crisis experienced by many of China's "lost generation" who are unable to find their proper place in the "normal world" and who are keenly aware of their own alienation. They feel uneasy about the past and the present, yet, at the same time, they hold no illusions about the future. Xu Xing's stories thus present a multi-dimensional picture of an absurd reality, the deeply rooted dilemmas of the human condition, and the ironies and ambiguities of a godless existence.

Like many of his contemporaries, such as Bei Dao and Yang Lian, Xu Xing has been influenced by a number of modern Western writers, including Nietzsche, Kafka, Camus, Sartre and Beckett. As in the case with many Chinese writers of "root seeking" (*xun gen*) literature, he also incorporates elements of Daoist philosophy into his work, thus successfully fusing Western modernity and Chinese tradition.

The literary techniques utilized by Xu Xing for his fictional situations are intrinsically linked to the themes of his stories which re-create the complexities of contemporary life. Xu Xing touches on a broad range of issues: distorted visions of reality, the imaginative universe involving a more subjective conception of time and space, illusions of the past, the disintegration of the self, the unrelatedness of the self to others, unconscious dreams of the future, the seemingly endless struggle to create dissension from the collective discourse, and heterogeneous modes of existence. These themes cannot easily be accommodated by traditional forms of realism. Xu Xing therefore adopts a more flexible literary vehicle that will give free range to his subjective imagination and allow him to capture the essence of the elusive and ambiguous reality of contemporary life. He thus relies heavily on modernist methods, such as symbolism and surrealism, to present sequences of fragmented images, fleeting impressions and disjointed notions.

The central theme underlying Xu Xing's narrative is the constant pursuit of the authentic expression of the individual self. It became fashionable during the 1980s for many Chinese intellectuals, particularly of the younger generation, to strive for greater personal freedom by breaking with convention and going against traditional constraints. The pursuit of individual subjectivity is an integral part of China's social transformation and modernization. It has its rational manifestation (though in a rather timid form) in the works of a number of contemporary philosophers, such as Li Zehou.[2] However, the most vivid and revealing expression of this "self-liberation" in a non-rational, more radical form is to be found in the works of China's young writers, where the revolt against tradition, convention and authority possesses an emotional intensity and intuitive immediacy.

The search for authentic individual expression in Xu Xing's work caused some controversy in intellectual circles, and his protagonists were dubbed by several cultural ideologues, most notably He Xin, as "'superfluous men' in China of the 1980s" (3–13). Xu Xing is not, in fact, the first Chinese writer to create a "superfluous man" image. Similar figures appeared in the work of several prominent Chinese writers, particularly in the two decades following the May 4th movement. Yu Dafu, for example, created some of the most celebrated "superfluous men" in modern Chinese literature (Ng: 96–117). Xu Xing's protagonist in "Variations Without a Theme" clearly shares some traits with Yu Dafu's "superfluous men" who are "overshadowed with this dream-like state of alienation, not knowing who they are, what they ought to do, or where they are heading" (*ibid.*: 100). However there are substantial differences. The protagonist in "Variations Without a Theme" does not sink into the mire of hopelessness as do Yu's "superfluous" heroes, who abandon all attempts at struggle. Iconoclastic, rather than cynical, Xu Xing regards the absurd world and the individual's meaningless existence as the norm or the reality one must unavoidably face, and he adopts an attitude of Daoist indifference to pursue the "real self" and individual subjectivity at a spiritual level, by transcending internal and external constraints.

---

[2] For more detail on the philosophical and literary pursuit of individual subjectivity in Chinese intellectual discourse during the 1980s see M. Lin, "Chinese Intellectual Discourse and Society—the Case of Li Zehou", *The China Quarterly*, 132 (December, 1992), pp. 969–98.

The Dilemmas of the Human Condition

Xu Xing strongly asserts the uniqueness of human individuality in his fiction. For his protagonists, being different from all others is essential to their sense of identity. The protagonist in "Martyr" proclaims: "… there is only *one* of me, and it is exactly this fact that makes me conscious of my existence." This search for a unique identity in defiance of collective uniformity has been the main focus of China's intellectuals in the post-Mao era. Xu Xing's emphasis on self-identity or individuality re-affirms the primacy of the self. One should establish one's essential being not by means of un-conditional submission to the faceless totality and uniformity of society, but through irreducible singularity. Thus, Xu Xing's protagonists cannot be easily classified. They are colourful characters who rebel against existing social norms and constraints. One of them even willingly allows himself to be admitted to a psychiatric hospital because of his "strange behaviour" and "crazed imagination".

A complex recurring theme in Xu Xing's stories is the implicit assertion that when one seeks to authenticate one's own existence, one inevitably comes up against a series of irreconcilable dilemmas, derived from tensions inherent within one's own nature. In "Variations Without a Theme" and "Story of a City", the narrators (as the protagonists) attempt, not altogether successfully, to overcome the conflicting desires to be happy and fulfilled individuals and at the same time to live as part of the social collective. In "Variations Without a Theme", the narrator tries to establish a genuine relationship with his girlfriend, Q, making compromises on several occasions and hoping that she will at least be one person in the world who might come to understand him. In "Story of a City", the narrator makes an even greater effort to build a stable relationship, finally marrying and settling down with his childhood companion, a girl he has loved for many years. But, in both stories, the consequences are bitter for the narrators, clearly revealing the impossibility of reconciling the deep dilemmas of the human condition. Such dilemmas persistently occur as themes in existentialist writings (Cooper: 110), at the core of which is the tension between the authentic individual and the social collective. Moreover, a deep dilemma is also manifested in man's limited existence—his finitude versus his inner desire for transcendence (a profound vision beyond his immediate reality which can endow his existence with a sense of purpose). Xu Xing's stories provide us with vivid illustrations of this dilemma. In "Variations Without a Theme", the narrator is basically a lonely man. Although the world he inhabits is crowded with people, he feels isolated: "I strolled casually out into the street. It was extremely busy, a boundless universe crowded with cars and people. But I felt terribly lonely."

The sense of loneliness and isolation experienced by the narrator is intensified by his estrangement from "others". One's inability to relate to others is a symptom as well as a root cause of social dislocation, a phenomenon explored by existentialist writers such as Sartre and Camus.[3] The irony of human existence is that, even though one yearns to relate meaningfully to others, the obstacles to achieving this seem insurmountable. The narrator is unable to remain in a state of solitude, because he needs others to relieve the unbearable loneliness of his social and psychological isolation to give him a sense of living again in society. At the outset, he manages to find companions to whom he feels he can relate. Ultimately, however, these relationships become the source of tension and conflict which not only fail to solve the problem of the individual's isolation but indeed hasten the disintegration of the self.

The narrators in "Story of a City" and "Variations Without a Theme" each take a female as an acceptable "other", someone to whom they can become emotionally attached. One, referred to throughout as Q in "Variations Without a Theme", is the narrator's girlfriend, and the other, referred to only as "she" in "Story of a City", eventually becomes the narrator's wife. In both cases, the

---

[3] D. Sprintzen, *Camus: A Critical Examination*, Temple University Press, Philadelphia, 1988, p. 53; J.-P. Sartre, *The Wall (Intimacy) and Other Stories*, tr. by Lloyd Alexander, New Directions, New York, 1969.

narrators' relationship with these women can be described as tense and paradoxical. They evidently love their respective partners and feel a strong emotional attachment to them. In "Variations Without a Theme", for example, the narrator imagines in his mind's eye a cosy nest, the home in which he will share many beautiful things with his girlfriend. There is no question about his sincere intention to get close to others, and, in fact, about his desperate need for others to offer him emotional comfort and provide him with a sense of his own existence. The problems that soon arise from the narrator's relationship with the girlfriend in one case and the wife in the other, however, are a manifestation of the unavoidable universal existential dilemma—the process of relating to others is often also the process of the disintegration of the self. One begins to lose one's own sense of identity and the freedom of self-relating when one is caught up in the complex web of inter-relationships.

In "Variations Without a Theme", the main point of conflict between the narrator and his girlfriend lies in the latter's desire that he should stop leading such an aimless existence and set himself some "proper", i.e. conventional goals. To the narrator, however, such striving is self-deceiving since life is like his short stories and his girlfriend's violin practice—it has no central theme, no content and no interconnections. Instead, it is nothing more than a series of contingencies. He does not know what he really wants, apart from things he already owns; he is not clear about who he is and, most importantly, he does not expect anything. His life consists of (in conventional terms) senseless or meaningless activities, like roaming the streets or drinking in bars. He abandons his studies at university, then refuses to join the mainstream as an establishment writer. Here, in the description of the protagonist's fragmented life, Xu Xing reveals that the rational totality and coherent unity of life experience, something accepted by many, is actually a myth; it presupposes a unitary discourse of cognitive rationality, moral certainty and aesthetic uniformity. The resulting version of a perfect society is lacking in tension and the self-conscious rational subject is assumed to be capable of making logical and sensible calculations in order to define the meaning and purpose of life. This self-confident and self-contained subject represented by Descartes'

Reason, and to a degree by Q in "Variations Without a Theme", constitutes the inner core of the modern Enlightenment tradition. And it is precisely this orderly, rational structure of life experience that is subverted or fragmented by Xu Xing in his stories.

The protagonists of both "Story of a City" and "Variations Without a Theme" can be perceived as the "decentred self", a concept used by certain contemporary Western scholars to signify the process of the "multiplication of self" or the "disintegration or loss of self".[4] More appropriately, it can be regarded as the dissolution of the old rational self—the mythical subject based on the Enlightenment concept of the coherent, self-contained individual. The deconstruction of the old self in Xu Xing's stories does not mean the total destruction of the self, but the re-creation of the authentic self, based on a rejection of the Cartesian subject consisting of the rational totality of coherent life experience. The fragmentation of this unitary structure of life experience is a deliberate device used by Xu Xing to achieve a literary expression of the authentic subject characterized by immanence, intensity, disorder and multiplicity.

In "Story of a City", the protagonist's motto is: "If you do nothing (*wu wei*), you're on the wrong road, and if you do something (*you wei*), damn it, you're also on the wrong road."[5] *You wei,* or consciously striving to achieve conventional goals, and its opposite, *wu wei* (non-willed action), or pursuing nothing in the conventional world, are key concepts in the Chinese Daoist tradition; Xu Xing utilizes them to convey an important philosophical theme—the Daoist dialectical attitude towards life which is symbolized by his protagonist. The boundaries between consciously striving to achieve

---

[4] M. Featherstone, "In Pursuit of the Post-Modern: An Introduction", in *Theory, Culture and Society*, Vol. 5, Nos 2–3 (June 1988); also C. Jencks, *The Post-Modern Reader* (see bibliography).

[5] One of the basic meanings of *qi lu* is "a side road off the main road", and has the connotation of divergence from the "mainstream". In Chinese society, where so much emphasis is placed on the importance of the social collective, to be away or apart from the "mainstream" (the main/right road—*zheng lu*) is to place oneself squarely on a "side road" or "wrong road" (*qi lu*).

conventional goals and pursuing nothing in the conventional world, and between the "right road" and the "wrong road" no longer seem so clear-cut, for everything one tries to do in terms of actively pursuing the meaningful in life often ends in unexpectedly absurd consequences. Any grand purpose one has is often no more than a self-created illusion or based on socially imposed conventions. Human effort is simply futile. Whilst still a child, the protagonist begins several years of wandering, but his journey through life, searching for some stable, comfortable final destination proves fruitless and brings only strange encounters and painful experiences, symbolizing the hopelessness of attempting to find some right way of living. Ultimately, refusing to strive for conventional goals (*wu wei*) may be just as meaningful as consciously striving for such goals (*you wei*), while the "right road" or "main road" (*zheng lu*) may essentially be no more right or proper than the "wrong road" (*qi lu*).

Xu Xing's interpretation of the Daoist concept *wu wei* is closer to Zhuang Zi's philosophical ideas than to Lao Zi's. Liu Huiying has observed:

> Zhuang Zi's ideal person should be defined in terms of a "non-existent" (*wu*) realm. With regard to spiritual consciousness, this ideal person is "selfless" (*wu ji*), a "non-achiever" (*wu gong*), and pursues "no fame" (*wu ming*); his life and conduct is characterized by "non-willed action" (*wu wei*), "waiting for nothing" (*wu dai*), and "uselessness" (*wu yong*); "selflessness" and "non-willed action" form the centre of a character model whose internal world is marked by "selflessness" and whose external world is marked by "non-willed action". (1992: 159)

Zhuang Zi's "selflessness" should not be interpreted as the complete elimination or negation of the individual self (subjectivity). Instead, what Zhuang Zi means by "selflessness" is actually the pursuit and discovery of the "authentic self" which transcends the conventional or mundane distortions and constraints imposed on the "pseudo-self" during normal existence. Therefore, Zhuang Zi's "the selfless", like the Existentialists' "authentic self", should be conceived as the highest stage of human individuality, the most ideal state of human existence, where one is free of all forms of alienation from the external world. It is also a perfect realm where one is able to go beyond all limits and constraints to attain real personal freedom and individual subjectivity.

In his stories, Xu Xing closely combines the traditional Chinese philosophical understanding of human individuality with the existentialist interpretation of the "authentic self", both of which aim at ultimate freedom for the self and regard the "other" or the social world as constituting the biggest obstacle to self-realization. Both also take personal autonomy and the inner ability for self-formation to be the core of individuality. However, unlike the Existentialists, Xu Xing clearly believes that the way to achieve personal freedom and authentic selfhood is not through "choice", but through ending conventional pursuits. There are few characters in his work who are able to accept this dialectical way of thinking. Q, in "Variations Without a Theme", is an example of those who regard consciously striving for conventional goals as being on the "right road", and throughout the story she makes several attempts to convince the narrator of the correctness of this attitude:

> It seemed as though Q wouldn't let be until she had dragged me up to a certain level; she was determined to turn me into someone like all the others, what I mean is, all those others who are pursuing a "career".

She asks him to sit for college entrance exams, telling him to "be a bit more realistic" and to have some proper plans in life.

But a clash becomes inevitable between Q and the narrator, since the latter wants nothing more than to be an ordinary person getting on with his own life in his own way. He certainly has no ambitions to be a great scholar. He is determined to reserve the right to keep his personality just the way it is, though it is not easy, perhaps even impossible, to achieve perfect freedom of self-identification. Once he begins to alleviate his sense of isolation by relating to others, the price he will eventually have to pay is the disintegration of his self-autonomy and his individuality. The narrator does his best to resist the pressures and temptations to abandon his own path for the easier route of conventional acceptance by becoming "one of them", but, ultimately, this results in a personal setback for him when his girlfriend terminates their relationship. So, he has achieved a greater level of freedom, but at the cost of being left alone once again. It seems the dilemma of self-identification and one's relations with others remains irreconcilable.

An interesting point raised in "Story of a City" is the daunting consequence of compromise on this issue. If one takes this piece as being in many ways a continuation of the narrator's life in "Variations Without a Theme", one cannot help wondering whether all his efforts to do the proper thing in conventional terms and to fit in with the mainstream by getting married and settling down is really a solution to the fundamental contradiction of the human condition. Judging by the evidence presented in "Story of a City", the answer has to be negative. Living together with his wife in a conventional setting becomes increasingly unbearable. He and his wife are engaged in an endless struggle to improve their living conditions—to obtain a larger room—which becomes an obsession with his wife and constitutes the only meaningful activity for the narrator.

The narrator in "Variations Without a Theme" still possesses the urge to write short stories and enjoys working as a waiter in a restaurant, but in "Story of a City" all these signs of active engagement in life seem to disappear completely. The boredom of everyday living becomes the hallmark of his married life. For the narrator in the first story, the most tedious time for him is his weekly rest day from routine work. During that day, he feels a particularly heavy psychological burden, since he faces what is for him the impossible task of deciding what to do. He admits that it really is a great relief to allow others to tell him what to do and make decisions on his behalf.

The inner fear that inhibits taking full responsibility for one's life indicates the deepest alienation and disintegration of the self. By losing his selfhood the individual no longer possesses the ability to self-relate, but, instead, is subject to external domination. It is also a clear expression of the senselessness or purposelessness of one's existence. This phenomenon is most clearly highlighted in "On a Side Road", when the narrator allows himself to be taken to a mental institution, even though he is not convinced about his supposed illness; from then on, it is the hospital staff that decide his routine and dictate what his proper behaviour should be. Passively, he allows them to feed him medications that put him into a comatose state for hours or sometimes days. Here, the narrator "no longer owns himself since, in one way or another, he has succumbed to a take-over by others" (Cooper: 109).

The Waiting Game

In Samuel Beckett's *Waiting for Godot*, the characters Vladimir and Estragon wait for Godot to come but, in the end, nothing happens, Godot never arrives, and their waiting is in vain. The endless process of waiting thus provides a revealing metaphor of the state and nature of human existence. "Waiting", as a universal phenomenon in human life, takes place every day, everywhere. But individuals have never had to endure the same quality of "waiting" as they now do in modern times, when "waiting" often becomes "boredom". So, it is not surprising that many modern writers have touched upon this issue in their work.

In Xu Xing's stories, "waiting" is a passive process of indifference and non-action. The protagonists do not care about what happens in the world any more, and they stop searching for a normal sense of purpose or meaning in their everyday life. For them, the conventional value system is no longer valid, and nothing can be treated seriously. The protagonist in "Martyr", when asked what he does, gives the blunt reply, "I don't do anything". His deep scepticism and cynicism towards life are also vividly expressed in the following dialogue with his old sweetheart:

> "If, for instance, we say that tomorrow everything will be destroyed in an earthquake, what will be of value? What will be worthless? What differences will remain between people?"
> "But you've still got to get on with things!"
> "In reality, there's nothing you can do, there's no time."
> "Why?"
> "Every path has already got someone walking on it far ahead of you. You'll be forever just starting out, even if you live to be a thousand."
> "Well, what has any significance?"
> "Enjoyment."

"What's eternal?"
"Depression."

In Xu Xing's stories, "waiting" is a central part of the characters' lives. We can distinguish in the narrative three kinds of waiting. The first is passively waiting without any clear idea or understanding of why one is waiting; the second is passively waiting with some kind of idea why one is waiting; the third is not consciously waiting for anything, but waiting at an unconscious level nevertheless.

In "Variations Without a Theme", the narrator can be said to experience the third category of waiting. At the beginning of the story he claims that he is waiting for nothing. The problem is, as he states it, that he does not know what he wants, apart from what he already possesses or what he already is, and this lack of a clearly defined purpose in his life is doubtless the reason why he is waiting for nothing. Moreover, the key point here is that he is not clear about who he is, so he actually has a problem of self-identity.

Feeling confused about one's identity is considered a modern disease. In "On a Side Road", one of the protagonists confesses: "I don't bloody know what kind of person I am." This confusion regarding one's own identity or selfhood reflects the deep crisis of existence; it is the symptom of an alienated world and a purposeless life. Accompanying this symptom are usually several others, such as intense boredom, the inability to manage one's own life and a feeling of uncertainty about one's spatial and temporal environment. All these symptoms are interconnected and reflect a deep sense of ontological dislocation, a modern disease which is comprehensively manifested in the three different kinds of passive waiting.

As the narrator is unconsciously caught up in the waiting process, time, as a standard unit or as a conventional sequence of events, no longer exists. Instead, fragments of memory, trivial details presented at random, imaginary scenes, and routine activities of an unrelated nature beyond the normal causal structure constitute this re-created time framework, blending the illusions of the past, the daunting realities of the present and the vague uncertainties of the future. In "Story of a City", the narrator as protagonist fuses the past with the present. The things that have happened in the past, those things that he encountered during his years of wandering, are utilized by him, as an important part of his history, to define his perception of present reality. The history of his life no longer comprises fixed given facts. Instead, it consists of the flux or stream of his individual consciousness based on personal memories and imagination.

A subjective or imaginative time-span is used to describe the strange relationship between the narrator and his future wife. She asks him why he left her to travel, why he returned after a hundred years and then waited another hundred years before coming to see her. In describing the relationship between the two characters, talking in terms of hundreds of years appears to be absurd on the surface. But in the context of the story, it is used to signify the fusion of the characters' personal psychological experiences with reality. Time is no longer a pre-given construct; it can be re-constituted in terms of one's memories of the past, one's perceptions of the present and one's expectations for the future, or, in sum, one's entire experience in the waiting process. (It can be argued that in the process of waiting, one's notions about time can be more subjective or imaginative.)

"Waiting" is a dialectical process. Though in "Variations Without a Theme" the narrator insists that he is not waiting for anything, since he is so unclear about what he wants and who he is, he is, in fact, still passively and unconsciously waiting. His "waiting for nothing", in the context of the story, is actually "waiting for something"; it is simply that the object of waiting has been lost, whilst the act of waiting itself remains. So, when the narrator claims that he is waiting for nothing, this is literally and precisely what he is doing: he is waiting, but with no clear objective to his waiting.

There is a relatively more active kind of waiting, the second kind, where one at least knows what one is waiting for. Belonging to this category is the narrator's wife in "Story of a City". She has a clear aim to move from their room of seven square metres to a bigger home, but the circumstances in society dictate that she cannot actively achieve this goal, and she must passively wait until fortune smiles upon her. The waiting temporarily becomes the entire content of her life. The narrator in this story is similar to his wife.

Fragmentation and Heterogeneity • 15

He too knows what he wants: a bigger home. Although both he and his wife initially try various means to achieve this, the narrator is finally told quite clearly by his bosses at work that he must "wait".

Waiting is a profoundly alienating process, as can be seen from this confession by the narrator:

> I'm a very patient person, I really love waiting. I have already got used to that kind of waiting, the outcome of which often leaves you not knowing whether to laugh or cry. For example, you wait for a beautiful girl to marry, and as a consequence, you wait eighty years. Just when you reach a hundred, she arrives. Surprised, you ask yourself how she could have become an old woman. As another example, you wait for a room; in the process of waiting you're not aware that you are slowly becoming a gross freak.

Waiting reflects the deep sense of impotence an individual feels when faced with an absurd world and estranged "others". It offers, in a sense, the best means of coping with hostile reality. As the narrator states: "... waiting brings me a feeling of consolation and conceals the dread I have about life, conceals my uselessness. Every time I feel useless and weak, I mockingly say to myself, 'Wait'."

Waiting is, in fact, a self-deceiving and self-defeating notion causing one to lose the most important dimension of human existence—the self-defining choice of making things happen and transforming one's own life. Just as in the play, *Waiting for Godot*, in which Godot, as the major motif of salvation, is a false hope, so the waiting game in general is based on human illusion.

In "Story of a City", the salvation motif for the narrator and his wife is their new home, a place that is bigger and better than their old room of seven square metres, which used to be a toilet. Having waited for a lengthy period, they are finally able to move into a room of seventeen square metres, which comes to them unexpectedly. It seems that Godot has finally arrived. Yet, after moving into their new home, they find they are too constrained by old habits to adjust to their new environment and automatically continue to use the same "dancing" movements they used in their old room because they lack a "new consciousness". One day, when the narrator's wife realizes she has again been using the old "dancing steps", it all suddenly gets too much for her. She throws herself onto the bed, wailing, "I can't stand it, I can't stand it. Let's just move back to our old place as soon as possible."

The end result of waiting can often be different from one's original hope. The thing you yearn for may never materialize, or something you do not expect may suddenly turn up. All the possibilities seem to suggest that waiting is a highly uncertain process in which anything or nothing could happen. However, according to the message conveyed in Xu Xing's stories, one thing is certain. The pain and agony generated by the conflict between habits entrenched during the waiting process and the new situation arising from the result of waiting can be as unbearable as the profound boredom experienced by those who play the endless game of waiting.

Knowledge, Individuality and Traffic Rules

In some of Xu Xing's stories, there exists a deep contradiction between an intuitive or spontaneous way of knowing and formal or conventional means of knowledge acquisition. These two modes of knowledge represent two very different ways of life. The properly defined, conventional route to knowledge is associated with official educational institutions, the schools, colleges and universities. It is also deeply rooted in the Confucian tradition that correct knowledge is always linked to officially sanctioned public discourse, of which conformity, universality and standardization are the most important features. Individualized, non-standard means of obtaining knowledge can constitute a serious challenge to the dominance of official knowledge discourse, which is closely interwoven with the existing power structure.

Xu Xing's sharp criticism of modern civilization and the conventional knowledge system is based on a Daoist attitude towards life. His protagonists reject the social pressure to be "civilized" and see all the social differences and categories in our conceptual system that are the products of human civilization as being, in fact, meaningless. There is no permanent or transcendent basis for human values and knowledge. According to one of the asylum inmates in "On a Side Road": "If you were to strip everyone and have them stand in front of you, naked, you wouldn't be able to tell which one was a king

Fragmentation and Heterogeneity • 17

and which one a beggar." The conventional boundaries between the normal and abnormal, right and wrong, are difficult to define. There is no sense in talking about what you know or do not know, since, when viewed from a different perspective, what appears to be a mystery or unknowable turns out to be, in fact, no mystery at all. Xu Xing's protagonists deny the importance of human reason, claiming that "Being rational is... painful. If you're rational, you can't achieve anything, so don't try and fool yourself you can."

Xu Xing's challenging of the supreme authority of modern reason is part of the intellectual effort to deconstruct the myth of cognitive and moral certainty by using cognitive scepticism and moral relativism to replace the absolute and transcendent structure of human life and the knowledge system. Contingency, irrationality and uncertainty are the hallmarks of Xu Xing's new world. Human life and the knowledge system, according to Xu Xing's protagonists, are essentially like a book without a proper beginning or end; it can be arranged or organized in an infinite number of ways, with a variety of possibilities, but it has no fixed logic or pre-determined structure.

The narrators in Xu Xing's "Variations Without a Theme" and "Story of a City" are university drop-outs, who seem to despise all modern and fashionable intellectual and cultural products. The narrator of "Variations Without a Theme" dislikes and ridicules the pretensions of the faithful followers of mainstream culture and society, his most acerbic comments being reserved for his former classmates, Present Tense (Xianzai Shi)[6] and Puppet Regime (Wei Zhengquan).[7] They write poetry using the most fashionable terms,

---

[6] The nickname Present Tense (*Xian Zai Shi*) refers to this individual's habit of using inappropriate tenses when writing poems in English. As a further meaning, it also indicates his predilection for all the latest fashions, in ideas, as well as in clothes, girlfriends, etc.

[7] This individual has a scar on his eyelid. Rumour had it that on one occasion, a girl he liked explained to him that she was not interested in him because of his scar. The term she used to refer to the scar, "jin bian" sounds the same as the Chinese for Phnom Penh, where there was installed what the Chinese government considered to be a puppet regime. So, the nickname Puppet Regime stuck. On another level, the

mix with foreign girls, achieve the best marks in the university examinations and go on to do postgraduate studies. They are the modern intellectual faithful. Although outwardly posing as such, they are in fact not anti-establishment, but, on the contrary, form a new but integral part of the establishment. What they pursue is not genuine individual expression derived from their own intuitive feelings and their connection with the pulse of life. They are motivated instead by the vanity of position and fame, and it is this that will inevitably lead them back to the establishment. All the "rubbish" mentioned by the narrator in his description of cultural phenomena will sooner or later be integrated into official culture and public discourse.

When the narrator and his wife move into their new and bigger home in "Story of a City", they discover they have a strange neighbour, a conscientious scholar. He is different from the narrator's university acquaintances; he has little or no contact with others and shuts himself away in his room, determined to solve the problem of entropy, a fundamental question of the universe. He has also set himself the task of working out the "mystery" of the number of pendulum swings made within a certain time by his wall clock. This reclusive scholar parodies those who believe themselves to be engaged in the serious pursuit of real knowledge, knowledge that will solve the important problems of the world and human life. In the dialogue between the narrator and his neighbour, they touch upon the subject of learning, and the narrator tells his neighbour that all the "proper" or "fashionable" subjects he once considered studying are actually meaningless. He says that what he wants to study now is "teasing cotton", which greatly disappoints the "master" of physics.

The most striking moment comes when the "uneducated" narrator points out to his neighbour that the solution to the riddle of the pendulum swings is incredibly simple. The pendulum moves sixty times a minute and all the neighbour has to do is count each swing

---

name gives some indication as to this individual's rather vain and pretentious nature, without any real basis in terms of his own abilities or level of popularity.

for himself. Hearing this, the "great scholar" suddenly loses his self-control, unable to believe that everything he has worked so hard and long to achieve is nothing more than a meaningless riddle he has created for himself. The implicit assertion appears to be that many seemingly great or important issues and problems in the arena of our publicly defined knowledge are in fact riddles we make for ourselves; moreover, we create a false sense of the importance of our pursuit of formal solutions to these senseless questions. This is why the narrator is certain that he could never be fully acknowledged as a "proper" intellectual in a university.

The way to create authentic self-expression or individualized knowledge, as implied in Xu Xing's stories, is to tenaciously pursue one's individuality, resisting external or internal temptations to compromise one's uniqueness or surrender one's self-identity to conventions, social norms or collectively-defined objectives. In the stories, the narrator uses various means to defend his individual way of life against the pressures of society to conform. One of the metaphors in "Variations Without a Theme" relates to the narrator's final description of himself as an absent-minded man who consistently fails to cross the road at the pedestrian crossing, or in other words, to do the sensible, conventional things that everyone else does. Although his girlfriend has finally left him because he refuses to conform to the socially prescribed values she tries to instil in him, he is determined to remain a happy man and reflects: "I'll still be the same as I am now, without rhyme or reason always happy and absent-minded. And when I cross the road, I'll never look to see whether or not I'm on the pedestrian crossing...."

Not using the pedestrian crossing on a busy road seems senseless. In fact, the narrator has already had a narrow escape in the scene where he is almost knocked down by a bus as he walks onto the road as if in a trance. The driver accuses him of being a lunatic, and in the eyes of several bystanders, the police, and even his girlfriend who is waiting for him on the other side of the road, he appears to be out of his mind. He does, in fact, sarcastically ask his girlfriend later to accompany him to the psychiatric hospital for a check-up. David Cooper sheds light on the likely reason for the crowd's reaction to the narrator's eccentric behaviour in his comment that:

The tribal dissident... will hardly be greeted by his fellows as a hero of authenticity. More likely he will be pitied as a man whose very identity is disintegrated by his attempt to stand out against the traditions which define a person's place in the cosmos. The opinions which he voices in opposition to the tribal traditions will likely be taken as symptoms of a sickness, or perhaps of pernicious foreign influences. (124)

Though he may be considered mad by others because he does not follow the traffic rules, it is the price the narrator is willing to pay for keeping his idiosyncrasies. It also indicates maintaining one's unique identity against the social collective is not an easy way of life, and can only be achieved by possessing a real sense of the absurd.

Xu Xing's portrayal of an idiosyncratic individual who rejects the conventional knowledge system and moral code can be interpreted as a subversion of the officially sanctioned public discourse which, as signified by the author, forms the cultural-spiritual apparatus that constrains the free development of the authentic individual. To use one of Lyotard's terms, Xu Xing's protagonist is actually involved in the process of "delegitimation" (Jencks: 139), which poses a direct challenge to the homogeneity of the official meta-narrative that legitimizes the dominant pattern of communication and, above all, the conventional mode of living to the exclusion of any form of dissension or alternative means of existence.

In undermining or delegitimating the collective consensus or authoritative criteria on truth, morality and aesthetic beauty, Xu Xing's narrators are championing the cause of heterogeneity in cultural-intellectual expression and in modes of living. The epistemological position taken by the author is clearly one of sceptical relativism, a position of "decanonization", which consists of "a massive 'delegitimation' of the master codes in society.... Thus, from the 'death of God' to the 'death of the author' and 'death of the father', from the derision of authority to revision of the curriculum, we decanonize culture, demystify knowledge, deconstruct the language of power, desire, deceit" (*ibid.*). In other words, the author's attitude towards knowledge is one favouring dissension and diversity over consensus and uniformity. It can be described as a cognitive and normative anti-authoritarianism that "requires our sensitivity to differences and reinforces our ability to tolerate the incommensurable. Its principle is not the expert's homology, but the inventor's paralogy" (*ibid.*).

Conclusion

Xu Xing's stories, like the life of his narrator, and the short stories written by the narrator in "Variations Without a Theme", appear to lack any central theme or logical connection. According to the narrator, stories, just like life, can be perceived in a variety of ways, but reason cannot be used to explain them. Modern life is like writing a piece of fiction—thus the distinction between reality and fiction becomes blurred. The search for a clear, well-defined theme and an intelligible logical structure in both life and fiction runs contrary to what we experience in our everyday existence.

Many Chinese intellectuals have sought in modernization a way to re-create a new vision of life, believing it to be a possible solution to the loss of meaning and purpose felt by many after the Cultural Revolution. Xu Xing, by contrast, questions all the basic notions of official discourse and this new vision adopted by the social mainstream. He scorns and mocks modernity based on the human conviction of the rightness of progress, knowledge and economic development, seeing it as an ailment of the human condition.

The philosophical stance Xu Xing takes can be summarized thus: the question of whether the world and human life is meaningful or meaningless is itself a senseless riddle created by humans. The theme of life is no theme, and the logic of reality is illogical. The best position to adopt is therefore one of Daoist transcendent indifference, or to desire and pursue nothing. Do not bother searching for some grand purpose or objective in your life since conscious striving for conventional goals and pursuing nothing in the conventional world are ultimately two sides of the same coin.

The interesting point is that although the narrator clearly wants to achieve some kind of Daoist transcendence, and mocking social norms and conventionally minded individuals in order to lighten his burden of absurdity so it won't crush him when he attempts to achieve it in a practical sense, he has some limited success but is ultimately unable to reconcile his Daoist-like attitudes with deeply alienated modern existence. In "Story of a City", his search for a new and bigger room, for example, symbolizes that the pull of mundane needs essential for his well-being in society will always inevitably bring him back to everyday life, which will almost certainly be in conflict with a state of Daoist spiritual transcendence.

In fact, it appears that ultimately, in terms of his practical existence, the narrator finds it impossible either to settle for living in the Confucian mundane world, or to have all his emotional needs met when following a more Daoist-like free-spirited life. He vacillates between the two, wandering for several years to satisfy the spiritual hunger in his soul, yet returning to society to satisfy his emotional need to feel deeply connected to other human beings. Perhaps it is only by vacillating between the two that he can keep his sanity. But in keeping this balance, he is walking a psychological tightrope, since his life is marked by a tension that can never be successfully resolved: the search for individual freedom results in loneliness, and the impulse for connection with others results in the stifling confinement of individuality.

This same kind of tension is also manifested in the deeply-rooted dilemma of Chinese intellectual discourse, and the various efforts by Chinese intellectuals to solve this problem is reflected in the wide spectrum of Chinese thought. The cultural legacy of Confucianism and Daoism, together with the new Western influences of the Enlightenment tradition, existentialism, modernism and postmodernism, comprise the main pillars of contemporary Chinese intellectual discourse, and Chinese intellectuals as diverse as Li Zehou, Bei Dao and Xu Xing draw on them as resources to reflect the state of modern life and modern existence.

Unlike his mainstream contemporaries, Xu Xing refuses to follow the old mode of literary realism, and its pursuit of ultimate values and the absolute meaning of human life. In his narrative, Xu Xing clearly denies the existence of totalistic, uniform and permanent solutions to the deep-rooted dilemmas of the human condition. For him, there is no linear chain of cause and effect underlying history and human activity. His carnivalistic interpretation of contemporary life, which "embraces indeterminacy, fragmentation, decanonization, selflessness, irony, hybridization" (Jencks 1992: 198), reveals the complexity of human existence, presupposing the individual's "participation in the wild disorder of life" (*ibid.*). Central to Xu Xing's deconstruction of the "rational self" is his uncompromising "anti system" stance (*ibid.*). There is a fundamental difference between Xu Xing's "decentred self" and the rational self defined in the text of mainstream intellectuals like Li Zehou, since the former transcends the rational framework of the latter's modern Enlightenment conceptual system. The synthesis of the pre-modern and the post-modern interpretations of the "self" in Xu Xing's stories has undermined the rational core of mainstream Chinese intellectual discourse. In this sense, Xu Xing's stories can be regarded as some of the earliest examples of post-modern cultural experimentation in contemporary China.[8]

---

[8] It should be acknowledged that, in some ways, Xu Xing's fiction is less mature artistically and technically, and reveals stronger traces of the author's emotional subjectivity—frustration, anxiety, restlessness, confusion, perplexity, disdain and anger—in comparison with the more controlled and dispassionate "author-less" narratives, produced by writers like Ge Fei and Yu Hua, that characterize the second wave of avant-garde writing in contemporary China.

Bibliography:

He Xin (1985), "Dang Dai wenxuezhong de huangmiugan yu duoyuzhe", in *Du Shu*, 11.

Ng, M. S. (1988), *The Russian Hero in Modern Chinese Literature*. The Chinese University Press, Hong Kong.

Cooper, D. E. (1990), *Existentialism*. Blackwell, Oxford.

Jencks, C. ed. (1992), *The Post-Modern Reader*. Academy Editions, London/New York.

Liu Huiyang (1992), "Xianqin rujia he daojia de lixiang renge", in *Xinhua wenzhai*, Vol. 1, No. 1.

On a Side Road

Every day they gave me a lot of medicine.

I took it.

I wasn't ill, but I still took it.

They put all kinds of questions to me, questions that were totally irrelevant. I gave them answers that were totally irrelevant.

One day, they gathered together a group of specialists to examine me. A woman doctor, whose eyes showed unswerving determination and whose nerves seemed unshakeable, asked me, "How have you been feeling recently?"

"There's nothing wrong with me! I'm fine!" I answered, my gaze unfocussed for several seconds.

She looked around at the others circling me. They smiled knowingly, as though I had told them a joke.

In my heart, I was smiling too, smiling at the game I was playing with them.

"Do you remember how you came to be here?"

"No."

She smiled again, seemingly satisfied with this answer. Perhaps their aim was not to let me know anything. Their greatest joy would probably be for me to become an imbecile, and that is why every day they sent a beautiful young nurse to give me those brightly-coloured tablets. After taking them, I always had the feeling that I was swimming, swimming in a bloody big sea of sticky glue. The end result was sinking, suffocation, loss of consciousness.

"You are ill, so you must rest quietly in order to recover. You shouldn't let your imagination run wild, am I right?"

"You're right!"

After walking away from me, they gathered around my fellow patient, A, who was a builder.

He was a really pitiful fellow. His greatest joy in life was when someone noticed him. He was one hundred percent a madman when people were around. So, as soon as the specialists surrounded him, he became excited.

The specialists asked him the same questions they had asked me. He replied with great drama, and was very long-winded, evidently wanting to reveal all.

"How are you feeling?"

"Not well. My head feels dizzy, my legs are weak, I can't eat, and...."

"Your appetite hasn't been good lately?"

"Mmm."

"Why is that?"

"The hospital food isn't good. There's not enough meat. My little sister cooks better."

His sister, sometimes accompanied by a sallow-looking fellow, always brought a lot of food when she came to see him. The food was left in the safe-keeping of the doctor, who gave it to him a bit at a time. He always offered me some.

He liked chatting with me, about his illness, about his work. As he chatted, with a trembling thumb and first finger he would put a cigarette to his trembling lips.

That's the kind of fellow he was! Though they said that my condition was more serious than his, it was, according to them, recessive.

My sufferings were too numerous, and my soul was fragile and sensitive, so that sometimes I thought that everything in the world was of concern to me. I am probably the scholarly type, the sort of person who often suffers with gastric ulcers and the like. Unfortunately, I also suffered from the illness they said I had, and, though I myself didn't think that was the case, they still brought me to this hospital.

He had also suffered a lot, but in his case, it was because nothing in the world was of any concern to him. His stomach was in perfect shape.

"If I ever get stomach trouble, it will definitely be from meat deficiency. When I was working, I even ate meat for breakfast."

His suffering was caused by the fact that nothing in the world was of any concern to him.

"I'm a bloody human being. But who knows, if I had fallen from some scaffolding one day and died, wouldn't I have lived for nothing? So, I don't work now. As soon as I went up on that scaffolding, I started to shake all over, so I was sent here. Actually, it's not bad, is it?"

"No, it's not!" I agreed with him, then asked, "What about your mom and dad?"

"They're dead. One from varicose veins, and the other from alcohol poisoning!"

When they were bringing me here in the ambulance, the siren blared continuously. I don't know what sort of injection they gave me, but afterwards my body wouldn't obey my brain. All I could do was listen with my ears. Each time the siren sounded, I felt as though someone were rolling a big metal rod from one side of my exhausted soul to the other, stopping when it reached the edge. And even though my soul was shaped something like a cube, say, the rod would never roll off, but go on, back and forth, until my soul had become a flat pancake.

The coarse canvas that kept shifting around under me was like a filthy shroud. The two aluminium carrying poles supporting the canvas pressed against my sides; the green paint had peeled on the handles, so that they looked like bald heads. God knows how many people had died on this stretcher.

"Stop the ambulance! Stop the ambulance!" I cried out. The others in the ambulance didn't react at all; they just sat quietly, their bodies swaying peacefully. No reaction whatsoever, so I didn't shout out again. I knew that in fact I couldn't have made a sound, otherwise, why was there no reaction?

My wife solicitously bent over me several times to see how I was. I knew that she was doing this so as not to let the others think that she didn't care in the slightest about me. I knew that she knew I was screaming, but she didn't show it. All I could see in her eyes was cruel delight at my suffering, as well as the hint of a wish that I would die on the spot. I was terrified.

During my lifetime, I have constantly received hints; everything that happens around me hints that I'm useless. I will never understand many, many things that I should understand. Sometimes a mass of thoughts would whirl chaotically in my head and finally sink into a heap of springy spider webs; then, those thoughts would struggle frantically, wanting to break free. Once, I felt that I had become a pile of thoughts, and all my clothes were sticking to me and wrapping me up. In a frenzy, I tore at my clothes, until I became utterly exhausted. Before I had finished, they gave me an injection and brought me to this hospital.

I shared a ward with A and B; we were fellow patients.

A became ill after a fright.

That day, he was working five floors up on some scaffolding. Suddenly, from more than ten floors above, came a loud crashing noise, followed by cries of "Aaagh!". The crashing moved downwards, and it was coming closer to him. Bricks, bags of cement and tools tumbled down, one after another. He was frightened out of his wits. He didn't dare look up and just shut his eyes and waited to see what would happen. After the crashing had stopped, he opened his eyes. He looked like a big egg in a big bird's nest; scaffolding, gangplanks and metal support frames were all tangled together. He looked through the cracks in this big nest and saw people rushing about, helpless; no-one noticed him. More than twenty ambulances went back and forth around the building site, smothering his cries for a full two hours. Only then did he hear someone outside call "Is anyone alive in there?" He quickly replied, "Yes! Yes!" Those two hours had been a narrow escape from death for him, because every now and then, from above, there was again the sound of crashing, and he would think that, this time, he must definitely be a goner.

"I went mad with fright", he said. "I rested at home for two months before going back to work. As soon as I got to the building site I began to shake again. I turned around and ran, calling out to my mates 'It's collapsing! It's collapsing!' The whole bloody site was in chaos, and after that they brought me here."

I was sick of hearing all that stuff. I picked up a book, but maybe because I had had too many of those brightly-coloured tablets, I couldn't focus on it. There was one line describing the launch of a satellite, and it was written in the language of the 1930s, which was half literary, half vernacular. I read it twenty times, but still couldn't understand it. So I put the book down and looked at my other fellow patient, B. He was scribbling madly with a red pen on a stack of paper, his hand movements swift and crazy.

"B, what are you writing?" I fancied a chat with him.

With a superior gesture, he held up the two corners of a sheet of paper with both hands. There was nothing on it. But perhaps there was something, who knows? Strange things can happen.

"Did you read it?" he asked.

"What?"

"What I've written!"

"Mmm. Not bad."

It was said that B was a writer. He was also in here because he had suffered too much. Once, he took a pile of his writings to all the publishing houses in the city. They all said he was crazy. To prove that he wasn't, he hurried back home and quickly leafed through all his journals, after which he became convinced that he was, in fact, mad. He took a small bag and went to the Public Security Bureau to give himself up.

"I'm mad," he said to a young policewoman.

"Mad?" She was shocked. "If you're mad, what are you doing here?"

"I've come to give myself up!" He put down his bag and, completely at ease, held out his wrists so he could be handcuffed. The policewoman quickly turned and went into a room to summon a couple of burly chaps who got him into a car and brought him to this hospital. After a series of tests, the hospital accepted him as a patient. As the policemen were about to leave, he gave a military salute as a gesture of thanks.

"It's nothing. It's our duty." From the way they said it, it sounded as though they hoped B would write a letter to the newspapers praising them. Then, laughing, they got into their car and left.

"Writers are the real bloody madmen. If not, where would they get so much to write about?" A began his offensive against B. "The book you're reading, for example. It's so thick. What's in it?"

"This book wasn't written by a novelist, it was written by a philosopher."

"What philosopher?" B's eyes lit up with excitement. He never missed the opportunity for an intellectual discussion. What a shame I couldn't concentrate and A was totally illiterate.

"Wiener's *Man, To Be Used As Man*.[1]

"What viewpoint does he hold?"

Then I explained to him that a person should be a person and not something else. He knitted his brow, deep in thought.

"Forget all that, B. Write about me! You'll definitely be able to write a book on my story. I'll tell it to you and you write it down, and I bet everyone will love reading it."

Ever since A heard that B was a writer, he kept pestering B to write about him. To catch B's interest, he was always telling us amusing stories. I liked listening to them.

"Okay," I promised on B's behalf. "Tell us about your bosses."

"Our bosses said it was forbidden to shit and piss up on the scaffolding where we were working.

"That's right. They never went up to do any work, so there was no need for them to shit and piss up there. They also said that if anyone pissed, they would be fined five *yuan*; if they shitted, it would be ten *yuan*. They also said that if anyone saw someone shitting or pissing up there and reported it, the money from the fine would go to them. After this, I was really a bit worried, because there was this idiot, X, who gave up working and instead walked about on the scaffolding watching everyone's backsides. If ever a couple of those backsides became too active, this guy could make

---

[1] Norbert Wiener (1894-1964) US mathematician credited with developing cybernetics. The book title is Xu Xing's own invention.

twenty *yuan*, more than he could doing a day's work. Our bosses kept their word.

"It was the middle of winter, and nobody wanted to come down for a shit or a piss. We were more than twenty floors up, and if you wanted to go, you had to go down on a pulley. So several dozen men made this unfinished building their toilet. When the building was finished, it was going to be for VIPs, maybe even foreign presidents. By that time, never mind shitting there, we wouldn't even be allowed in the door. With these thoughts in mind, my mates would open up an empty cement bag on the glazed tiles and squat there to have a shit. When they had finished, they would lift up the four corners of the bag, clasp them all together, and with one heave, throw the bag out of the window. If you ever visit our building site, and see any bulging cement bags, whatever you do, don't stand on them.

"Whenever I think about that, I feel happy. There are a lot of plush guestrooms in that twenty-five storey building, costing, so I'm told, several hundred *yuan* per night for a room. But it doesn't matter how much bloody money it costs, or who lives in it, because in spite of all that, my mates have had a shit there."

"That shows a massive contrast between your depressed psychological state and contemporary civilization," said B, coldly.

A looked aghast.

"If you write that in your book, no-one will bloody understand it, and it's not what I said."

B hated the conventional world and its ways. Whatever I or A said, he always brought it up to a higher philosophical plane, a rational plane, and added totally irrelevant arguments. A was most envious of scholars; B's sophistry often left him palpitating with fear.

"Contemporary civilization?" A blinked. "I'm no bloody civilized man. What do I want with civilization? That boyfriend of my sister's—and if things go badly, he might become my brother-in-law—says, you're either civilized or you're a savage.

"I don't know what a savage is. Maybe it's those men and women who go around naked, covering only their private parts with animal skins. If that's what it is, I'm not a savage either. I don't bloody know what kind of person I am.

"Once, I spat in the street, and a group of blokes who were there to make sure the city stays clean wanted fifty cents from me. I knew it wasn't right to spit in the streets, but when some genteel old lady began telling me I wasn't civilized, I was ecstatic. I'm not a bit civilized. What do I want with all that? If I were civilized, would I be able to squeeze into a room of eight square metres with my sister who's barely twenty years old? What's civilized about that? I'm thinking about finding someone to pay a fine for that!

"Oh, after I'd finished saying this, those blokes were delighted. They decided not to fine me, and they let me off with just wiping up the spittle. Maybe they also have to share a small room with a teenage sister, perhaps they even share the same bed! Maybe when they had heard what I had to say, they realized that they themselves weren't bloody civilized.

"I have a lot of phlegm. I can't help it, I smoke too much, and I always roll bloody big fat ones!"

I didn't want to hear any more, and I covered my head with my quilt.

My wife came to visit and brought me some cigarettes. She was there to see if there was any chance of my being discharged from the hospital in the near future, so that she could make some arrangements.

The long, narrow corridor was like a rope you'd use to hang yourself. Every day, B walked up and down it briskly. Whenever he met someone, he always asked urgently, "Have you got a cigarette?" His extreme impatience always made you feel that the world should really be one big cigarette factory.

While he was off somewhere, I took the opportunity to look through his pile of papers. On them were written indecipherable symbols, and a footnote said, "extra-terrestrial writing". Under each line of this "extra-terrestrial writing" was a Chinese translation in brackets. I copied the translation down as follows:

They eat food that has been cooked by fire. They wrap cloth around themselves. Everything they do is geared towards eating and sleeping (they always sleep in pairs, one they call a man, the other they call a woman). Even though eating and sleeping is all there is, they themselves do not know this, so they also have a lot of other things. They are divided into different religions and ideologies; and they have their own spaces, which are called countries. They slaughter each other, inform on each other; they have hair and skin of different colours; they can become ecstatic or down-hearted over nothing at all; those of them who write are called "intellectuals", those who sit in big, ugly, hippo-like cars are called officials or wealthy; money is a piece of paper that can influence their mood, those with a lot of money are called wealthy, and those with little money are called poor. If you were to strip everyone, and have them stand in front of you, naked, you wouldn't be able to tell which one was a king and which one a beggar. You would only be able to distinguish them as male or female, fat or thin, old or young.

Perhaps you would also note that on this small ball of earth and water, people die and live, live and die, in cycles. But, the people on this small ball of earth and water aren't even aware that all their rushing around is just for this cycle of life and death. Some of them are veritable sexual floodwaters or vigorous erections....

Rumour had it that it was precisely because he had written this kind of novel that he had become my fellow patient. I read it, dumbstruck, and couldn't believe I was reading such things. Perhaps I imagined them, and, at that point, for the first time, I agreed with the prognosis of the woman doctor with the look of unswerving determination. I was bloody mad!

I rushed out of the room, holding those pages and wanting to confirm that I had really read what I thought I had read. B looked up, rushed over and dragged me back into the ward: "I'll confirm it for you." He cleared his throat and began to read, "There was not a single cloud in the azure sky. A beautiful young girl stood beneath the blue sky. She wore a pink dress. Her curved eyebrows were like crescent moons. She said: 'I love you, I do love you....'"

"No! No! That wasn't it!" I cried out, crestfallen.

B's eyes lit up, half questioning, half surprised. "What's up with you?"

The nurse came to give me an injection and my medicine, after which I knew nothing.

I didn't wake until the following evening, and, in a daze, I heard A providing B with source materials.

"I said, I'm not civilized...."

It was that same old bloody stuff again. I rolled some toilet paper up into two balls and stuffed them in my ears, then quietly thought my own thoughts. After so many years had passed, I still kept on going back to those memories....

I thought about the time when I was a child and had a picture book. Only from the spine of the book could you tell that it had once been quite thick. The beginning and the end had been ripped out, leaving only a few pages that were barely hanging on the binding. One day, I cut all the remaining pages out, and then cut off all the page numbers, then I mixed the pages up, and began to read. I read it time and time again, never feeling bored with it. After reading it through, I would rearrange it, so that each time it had new content. I really loved that book, and I carried it around with me every day. I let my little friends read it, but no-one could understand it. Only I knew the stories in it, and I could relate them from start to finish, though I didn't tell them to anyone. On one occasion, I was reading my book in the park, when an old man with a white beard walked over and, full of good intentions, helped me to put the book back together again properly, and then read it out beautifully from start to finish, so as to let me know what a story with a proper beginning and end was. I conscientiously read through the book, but discovered that it no longer interested me and no longer seemed precious, so I threw it away and went home, crying and broken-hearted.

I thought about those events over and over again until after dinner, when everyone went off to watch television. A, B and I didn't have much in common, but when it came to watching a TV quiz show, we were unusually on the same wavelength. We all wanted to use this boring program to determine the extent of our illness. Before the program started, there was a stream of ads. A really liked watching these, and used them to exercise his brains. For instance, the moment the announcer said: "Medicine X... Medicine X. Please use Medicine X," he would immediately change it into an advert for DDVP.[2] Imitating the announcer's voice, he would say,: "Can't forget your troubles... can't forget your troubles. Please use DDVP!"

Some professor in the hospital was just putting the final touches on a new cure. He had come to the conclusion that watching television could help a mentally sick person to recover, because you don't have to think when you're watching. This has a calming effect on the nerves and is also an effective method of birth control. It was said that he was writing up his hypothesis to present at an international academic conference on mental illness.

The quiz show started, and A, B and I tensed, our hands firmly gripping our cigarettes, itching to have a go.

"How many cells does a honeycomb have? How many matchsticks does a matchbox contain? Which coin is the thickest? What makes more noise, a gong or a drum?"

We sat there like idiots, never imagining that the smiling woman presenter would ask such hard questions. We had thought she would just ask a few simple ones.

I thought again to myself, I am mad! Because normal people must know the answers.

"Damn it! Why doesn't she ask how many bricks are needed to build a four-storey building?" A shouted.

B was rocking back and forth on his chair, looking a little indignant: "She should have asked something on Chinese civilization, like, do the Chinese people come from Antarctica or the Arctic Ocean, or have the Chinese evolved from apes or toads?" He rushed forward to smash the television set, but a group of patients seized him and were grappling with him on the ground. I got out of the way, and watched the scene from a distance, my eyes full of the blue

---

[2] DDVP, a powerful pesticide, has been implicated in numerous suicide cases in China in recent years.

and white stripes of the patients' hospital clothing—straight vertical stripes that had now become a twisted, distorted mass....

The woman doctor thought that my illness had stabilized, and she allowed me to go home to see what was happening there. I don't know what I was supposed to go home to see. It was a two-hour journey from the hospital to my home but I was hoping that I would stay forever on the road, that the sky on my journey would be forever blue. In the bright sunlight, everything was sharply defined. No matter what happened in the human world, the sun would still rise as usual; if the world was destroyed, the sun would still rise as usual; if I were to die, the sun would still rise as usual; if I were to become mentally ill, the sun would still rise as usual. I felt that my life was so insignificant and fragile that I couldn't sustain myself....

Human life is so fragile. On what do people still base their belief that they are strong and powerful?

The weather wasn't at all warm. The streets were covered with filthy ice, ice devoid of any brilliance. I closed one of my eyes, and moved my head from side to side, so that I could observe the distant hazy warmth of the world. In the restless noise of the city, petty thieves, coolies, townspeople, pedlars, debris, everything, were exposed as insensate cold phenomena. I wondered whether there really were, as B described, super-intelligent bright-eyed creatures who would gaze in awe at all this from another world? After thinking about it for a while, I was still at a loss. What was all this tomfoolery anyway?

A middle-aged guy with an out-of-town accent was shivering in the cold. From time to time, he stamped his feet to stop them freezing. He was pointing to a large abacus on the wall, and explaining to the people gathered around him about some "high-speed scientific method of calculating", until he was hoarse and exhausted from his exertions. Below the abacus hung a piece of red cloth, on which was written something about something being for free.

Why isn't anyone like him ever brought to the hospital? I thought he would make a very witty fellow patient, and I would definitely in all sincerity ask his advice about using the speediest way to calculate when the world would end....

The hospital cured some people, calming their senses but destroying their desires and emotions; some people were made worse, and they became solemn and serious.

B had begged me to buy some magazines for him, and had listed a whole lot of titles. I walked over to a bookstall and leafed through a few. A novel among them caught my interest. I stood for some time in the cold windy street reading it, but in the end I couldn't tell whether the characters in the story were Chinese or foreigners, because the protagonists all had foreign nicknames, like "Adam", "Eve" and "Mona Lisa", to differentiate them. They also danced gipsy dances and sang Russian folksongs. The novel mentioned Picassos hanging on the wall, and the music being in Z-major, K-minor, and H-major, to point up the writer's profound cultural accomplishments, and the fact that he well-versed in things both Chinese and Western. But when I looked at it again carefully, I discovered that the hero was called Zhang Facai, and the heroine, Li Debao. They weren't called "Mary" or "John" after all.

I leafed through another book, and came across the words "The sound of Beethoven's magnificent and grand *Eroica* started up nearby…." I couldn't stand it and quickly shut the book.

I wanted to go back to the hospital and, with all my heart and soul, I wanted to tell that woman doctor with the determined expression that I acknowledged my madness. I decided to cooperate fully with her treatment, so that I could restore my faculties sooner.

I also thought about the fact that when my mother gave birth to me she wanted me to be a good person, yet despite all my efforts I hadn't succeeded; on the contrary, I had so easily slipped into madness. But it doesn't matter. If there really is that bright-eyed alien out there on another planet, what difference would goodness or madness make to him?

If you think in this way, then it doesn't matter. It doesn't matter. It really doesn't matter.

I walked along in the icy cold wind. I wanted to go home. Home was always familiar. In the days before I was taken to hospital, each time that I snapped out of one of my trance-like fantasies, I was often surprised to find myself lying in bed at home, staring at the ceiling.

After a quick investigation, I would find that either my face was covered in tears or that I was dancing around in ecstasy. Then I wouldn't investigate further. I didn't want to know why I was crying, why I was laughing. I just thought about the fact that I was at home, a home with a wife. Often, when I accidentally broke things like ashtrays or wine bottles, she would rush over and clip me on the ear, the look on her face full of disgust and disappointment.

"So what if I hadn't broken it?"

"Then we could use it."

"So what if we could use it?"

"We wouldn't need to buy a new one."

"So what if we have to buy a new one?"

"We won't have any money."

"So what if we don't have any money?"

"We'd have a difficult life."

"So what if we have a difficult life?"

"We'll be poor."

"And if we weren't poor?"

"We'd have a comfortable life."

"So what if we don't have a comfortable life?"

"If you don't want to live comfortably, then just die!" She finally lost patience.

"So what if I die?"

"If you die, you'll become dogshit."

"And if I'm not dogshit?"

She didn't say any more and just stared at me with her terrible eyes. I could tell from those eyes that she wanted to kill me.

From then on, I loved playing this game with everyone, and most of all I loved playing it with guys who were on the eloquent side. I found that none of them was a match for me, and all they could do was stare at me with eyes that weren't too much better than my wife's....

I got infinite pleasure from this game and I loved it as much as I had loved the book I had when I was little. As soon as you see some other aspect or point in all these unknown mysteries and realize that there is actually nothing to them, you can feel completely content.

I arrived home at last. My wife was doing some cooking with a big, tall fellow, and they were chatting and laughing together. I told him to get lost. He went off, but before going out the door, he clipped me around the ear. My wife watched, gloating over my misfortune.

I thought long and hard about what they might have been up to. After a while, I decided that whether they were up to this or that didn't matter. So what if they were?

Everything I know, I don't want to know, and everything I don't know, I have no way of knowing....

Martyr

He stood alone on one side of the street. Finally, a truck rushed past, and from the other side, amidst a crowd of people who were surging across, came the sight of a familiar face. She quickly brushed past him.

He turned around and found that she had also turned around at the same time, her movement hesitant and slow.

They had met again.

It was evening in the city; the light misty rain obscured the familiar sight of the fiery setting sun as it slowly slid behind a cluster of buildings; it was a sight that engendered feelings of melancholy and listlessness. The towering buildings in the distance seemed to be surrounded by a layer of misty haze.

Their meeting once again, in the rain, on a pedestrian crossing, was reminiscent of the night they parted ten years ago.

She thought to herself, somewhat jokingly: the world is nothing more than a machine, an old-fashioned and obsolete machine that makes people split up, meet again, split up again, and meet yet again.

He hadn't changed at all; he was exactly the same as he had been ten years ago. He was casually dressed; his pale face radiated intelligence and a certain look of cunning clearly evinced his abhorrence of the conventional world, all of which made her feel as though their parting of ten years ago was only yesterday.

"Are you married?"

"I was." He looked her up and down. "Is that the first thing you want to know after ten years?"

She stood there uneasily. He could still suddenly make her feel unsure of herself.

Sometimes she wanted him to be like this, suddenly revealing all the mysteries that everyone thinks should be kept absolutely as mysteries. Letting you know all the things you want to know, letting you see everything you want to see is, after all, quite exhilarating.

"I'm not really bothered. I'm not really bothered what I know first and what next."

"How about you?"

"What about me?" She couldn't be like him, unthinkingly keeping him guessing.

"Are you married?"

"I was." She also wanted to mention her child but hesitated and said nothing. Then she quickly asked herself, why didn't she mention it? People are really strange!

Only at this point did she carefully observe him. She thought, ten years have gone by, and now I can categorize him as a particular kind of person. Well, what category can I put him in?

No-one wants to live according to their real natures, so life is exhausting, she thought.

For instance, scholars like the idea of "real men", and they try to pretend to be coarse "Robin Hood" types, while the incredibly vulgar "Robin Hoods", who will never be scholars, adopt the superior and arrogant airs of learned men.

He had a sharp chin and sunken cheeks; from above his eyebrows to the short, slightly curly hair along his hairline was a rounded curve; his large, broad forehead was like a woman's, smooth and without wrinkles. If human characteristics were revealed only on foreheads, there was no way he could have evolved from apes.

"You look as depressed as ever. How are you doing?"

"Sometimes I'm OK." His replies were all very short and left her guessing. Was their meeting again a happy or a sad thing for him?

He probably intuited what she was thinking. "Let's go for a drink! We often used to go for a drink together."

"We don't have umbrellas."

"We never did." He looked at her, his expression complex, emphasizing the two words "never did".

She recalled their parting of ten years ago; on that rainy evening, he dragged her off to find a bar. The two of them, foot-weary and exhausted, covered several long streets.

"Only bloody hell never closes." He went along, cursing. They had been together the whole day, but had talked very little. Both had premonitions about what the end result was going to be. They finally found a small bar. Inside the sound of people playing finger-guessing games was deafening. The bar girl had a look of despair and disgust. Only an old balding attendant with a cigarette behind each ear was chatting with her.

She had wanted to tell him that she never came to these places, but, because she didn't want to hurt his feelings too much just before they broke up, she didn't say anything.

He stared blankly for a while at the dark red price list on the wall, then ordered a couple of dishes. She recalled that they drank a lot that day. She herself stared vacantly out of the window, not seeing anything. Then she remembered noticing an elderly couple outside, with blank expressions, huddled together under an umbrella, walking at a stroll, placing their feet carefully in the dim light of a streetlamp. The muddy water that splashed up left the bottoms of their trousers wet.

It was raining very hard. She reflected that by the time she got home, her clothes would be soaked through.

Only old folk never forget anything. They don't forget love, they don't forget to take an umbrella....

"I would rather just dream, but unfortunately even my dreams are colourless."

Now she felt that she could forgive everything he had said ten years ago. Naturally, she could also forgive herself, because at that time they were both too young.

"Don't be too self-confident, it will constrict you."

"If, for instance, we say that tomorrow everything will be destroyed in an earthquake, what will be of value? What will be worthless? What differences will remain between people?"

"But you've still got to get on with things!"

"In reality, there's nothing you can do, there's no time."

"Why?"

"Every path has already got someone walking on it far ahead of you. You'll be forever just starting out, even if you live to be a thousand."

"Well, what has any significance?"

"Enjoyment."

"What's eternal?"

"Depression." He drank deeply. "This is strong stuff." He brought the glass down fiercely on the table; some of the liquid spilled and he casually wiped it with his sleeve.

"You should choose a different path."

"This isn't the bloody kind of world where you can just change paths. There are no paths that haven't already been walked on by someone."

"But as you're living, you've still got to carry on walking!"

She was getting impatient, and he tactfully refrained from saying anything more.

Every day she spent with him made her feel heavy, even though he was clever and unpretentious. He wasn't like some people who seem to be this or that, but in reality are stupid, stupid to the point of being hypocritical or cunning, just like a lot of people who think themselves generous yet in reality wouldn't even sacrifice a hair to help anyone else.

He was not stupid, oh, not at all! She believed that only stupid people pretend to be something they aren't. Perhaps those who are good at acting are generally regarded as "clever people", but she believed that, with her discerning eye, she could see through them all. When she had first begun to understand something of boys, and she and her girlfriends were all having a laugh together, they would ask her what kind of boy she would "look for". She replied by saying that she wanted someone who "wasn't stupid".

"I have to leave you. Whenever I'm with you, I'm always at sixes and sevens."

"And if you're not at sixes and sevens, what then?"

"Don't always use that big philosopher tone of voice. If everyone were like you, the world would come to an end."

"But actually there's only *one* of me, and it is exactly this fact that makes me conscious of my existence. I don't know how wave after wave of human beings who are indistinguishable from each other are able to affirm *their* existence."

"It's precisely this standard of right and wrong that has made you become neither one thing nor another."

Whatever happened, she firmly believed that in this universe there existed a variety of rational, normal standards of right and wrong. The reason why she wanted to leave him was because she felt he would destroy his life. Was he right in what he said? A person who doesn't want to be a general won't make a good foot-soldier, but then why are there many thousands times more of the best foot-soldiers than there are generals?

Maybe nothing really does last forever; except hope, hope that torture is eternal. If there was no hope, then there would be no torture, but what kind of life would that be? She couldn't imagine.

They returned once again to that small bar of ten years ago. It had now become a fair-sized restaurant. The dark red price list on the wall, the old, balding attendant and the sound of finger-guessing games had all disappeared, replaced by red sofas and soft chairs, and neatly-dressed waitresses with nice faces.

They sat in silence, each looking at the other with an unfathomable gaze, as though each wanted to unearth something that was in the other's heart.

He noticed she was still wearing square-toed strap shoes showing a large part of her foot: the curves of her ankles were soft and undulating, exquisite and smooth. You could imagine the delicate, plump feet inside the dark blue stockings. He felt a rush of warmth in his heart.

They argued that day ten years ago because they had been talking about marriage. She was sitting on the sofa, the straps on her shoes undone. With an effort, she tried to calm herself. Her small unstockinged foot was swaying slightly, her shoe rhythmically hitting against her heel. On reflection now, he thought that this movement had been exaggerated, unnatural.

She placed the book she had been holding onto the coffee table beside her, and, as she did so, her hand trembled slightly. He remembered that she had been reading some banned "capitalist humanist" novel.

He was worried that his words would hurt her, and wondering how he could console her, so for a time he just sat silently facing her.

A large black cat walked towards her, meowing. She stroked its back, and it jumped onto her lap, where it curled up. The hand stroking the cat seemed so pale, so delicate.

"Tell me what benefits marriage brings?"

She bent over to fasten her shoe straps, then suddenly stood up and walked towards the door. The cat, which had been snoozing, was thrown onto the floor. It screeched and slipped away.

"What's wrong?"

"I've been a heavy drinker and I've wrecked my stomach. Now if I drink a bit more than I should, I get stomach pains."

"Ah, so something about you has changed over these ten years?" she smiled.

"I've aged."

"What do you do now?"

"I don't do anything. How about you?"

"What?"

"What do you do?"

"I write novels. I'd like to write about you," she said, half joking.

"People won't believe that you're writing about someone who's Chinese, because everyone says that it's only foreigners who have plenty to eat and drink, and then, having enjoyed to the full the fruits of civilization, feel awkward and curse modern life, as though this bloody world was made just for them. So many shits and prostitutes who, while putting up memorial arches for virtuous behaviour, deliberately give you the cold-shoulder and use a lot of old women's gossip to insult you, in the hope that you'll live and die alone...."

"If I don't want to, I won't live and die alone, neither will you, because things are not the same as they were ten years ago."

"But you're still the same." He gazed at her, his eyes shining....

"I'm not the same. I have something to prove my existence."

"What?"

"My son."

"A child? What can a child prove?"

"He'll grow, he'll be full of hope, he'll be someone who won't suffer too much sorrow."

"Probably superfluous."

"Look, life is ugly, and people feel helpless in the face of this ugliness. All they can do is expose it and their own helplessness, and mock it, just like you.... Only this ugliness is superfluous.... Anyway, my son won't have any dark or gloomy thoughts, otherwise, I would rather he were blind and deaf."

"Well then, you could keep a dog, why does it have to be a human being?"

"I won't allow you to insult my son like that!"

They both stood up. She was a little hysterical. Everyone turned and looked at the two of them. A group of young lads, who were drinking beer and reeling all over the place, called out: "Hey! Go on, go on! Let's have some fun!"

A waitress came over.

"Your bill," she said coldly.

"Fine, only first it looks like I'll have to go and sell some of my blood," he said, self-mockingly.

She paid the bill, collected her things and walked out with him sheepishly following after.

They were both walking towards his home, a small broken-down room in a nearby suburb. Ten years ago they had emerged from this small room, only to part....

He had felt that life was dull and boring.

She had felt that the days with him were also dull and boring.

"You can't call this a home." Up to that point, she had remained single, and her understanding of what a home should be was abstract and distant.

"Let's do it!"

She didn't say anything as she slowly undressed, and unfastened the straps on those wonderful shoes.

He had an indulgent look on his face as his hands tremblingly caressed her body.

"Was it good for you?" she asked, after they had finished.

"Not the best."

She felt he had been frenzied and rough and made her body hurt all over. "For you, there's never anything that's just perfect, is there? But there are some things that you'll take to extremes, if you carry on like this. Like getting drunk, for instance."

"All I have are feelings."

"But feelings always mean trouble. That's why you're always suffering…."

"Being rational is even more painful. If you're rational, you can't achieve anything, so don't try and fool yourself you can."

She began to dress quickly. The square-toed shoes that looked as if they belonged to a child seemed to have stretched and got bigger, so that when she walked, they made a flapping sound.

"Ah, it's the end." He was half leaning against the bed, and lighting up a cigarette. A contented feeling came over him, and he gazed blankly at the clothes thrown carelessly on the back of the chair.

"The end of what?"

"Nothing," he said, casually.

"It's the end of you."

"You're right. The pity is that this world won't end with me."

She came to an abrupt stop, not knowing why she was walking with him, walking in this illusory light misty rain….

"I have to go home." She discovered that a main road going alongside two railway tracks stood in their path. In the distance, was the rumble of a train.

He stared at her, but she felt that there was nothing in his expression.

She walked home along the main road. The train was getting nearer. She turned to look at him, and thought, if life was such a burden, why did he carry on? If he had the courage of a real man, he should choose death and sacrifice himself for his principles. Even though that's stupid.

He also turned to look at her.

"Go on, go away...." The clanging of steel and iron replaced his hoarse shouting.

The train went past. Briefly, she saw a young man, his face pressed against the train window, looking at the wind and rain outside.

The train was carrying forward people, expectations and hopes, the heavy burden of life. Perhaps it would stop at some stage, then go on with a roar.

She walked on, woodenly, reflecting that their meeting again had cleared a ten-year debt of lovesickness. The rain was getting heavier. Ahead, there was what appeared to be a little village, the outline of which could be seen through the sheets of rain. She began to walk more briskly, wanting to get out of the rain and be in a place where there were lights and people.

On the outskirts of the village was a donkey, tethered under an old elm tree since who knows when. It was soaked through and kept pawing the ground restlessly. Dim lights shone from the windows of every house. She suddenly realized that today she was supposed to go and pick up her child. On the last occasion, as she was sending her son off, he kept chattering on about a story his teacher had told him, a story of a child who told lies. Life still has hope, she thought. There are teachers who hope children won't tell lies any more. Life is good after all. As she became calmer, she felt tired, and vaguely hoped that it wouldn't rain again tomorrow, that tomorrow would be a clear, sunny day....

Variations Without a Theme

Fortunately, I'm still holding a seed which has lost its sweetness—a bitter-tasting core
Fortunately, tomorrow morning I will set off to climb a mountain
I want to bury it
In the most secret cavern, and wait till next year when it will come to life
And put forth flowers and wafting fragrance. The tree will exude sweetness
The tree will be full of yesterdays
In the depths of the mountains where the sound of birds is never heard.

I

Perhaps I really have no prospects. Perhaps. I really can't work out what else I should want, apart from everything I already have. What am I? What's worse is that I'm waiting for nothing.

Perhaps each person is waiting, waiting without rhyme or reason, always believing that something will happen to change their whole life. But they're unable to say what they are waiting for.

Really, I'm waiting for nothing. In saying that, I'm not trying to tell you that I'm anything out of the ordinary. In fact, in another sense, I'm too well aware that I have needs; I need to eat, I need to work.

Apart from these, what's fashionable does not concern me.

If I were to die suddenly, what would be the repercussions? Probably the same as if an ant died. Perhaps Q would be upset for a few days but she'd get over it soon enough. She'd get married, and as she carried on her so-called career, she would lose no time in finding pleasurable things to do. And she would offer all that sweetness and charm that had once been for me to another man.

Since the person I love most would be like that, then who would feel that I was worth anything?

I don't like the incomprehensible music Q plays. I have heard that Debussy often liked to write music without a theme. Even though at times I have been mad about Tchaikovsky (and some others), I don't like the monotonous sound of any single instrument, apart from the trumpet. The trumpet is also monotonous, but it's always quite lively, so it makes you feel a bit better, with all that pushing and pulling.

It's a pity Q doesn't play the trumpet. I really overlooked this fact when we were caught up in our passionate love affair. Even though she plays a violin made by a famous Italian, and even though it is several hundred years old, I still can't stand all the finger exercises, sound tests, tuning, and things like that. It really is too damn themeless. Being themeless is not so bad, but not having any content or coherence, well…. Apart from the whole thing being rather formal, it's really a bit like the stories I write. I am often left feeling upset and uneasy.

I wonder why she can't just pick up her violin and play something pleasant for me. Instead, it's always a long period of noisy preparation, which immediately turns me right off, just like when you're busily biting on an apple and suddenly bite into a big, thick, fat worm.

She said I didn't understand. Perhaps I really don't understand. And then she left. Most probably she's gone off again somewhere to adjust those four precious strings. But she will come back. I do believe she'll continue to love me.

Some time ago, when we were walking slowly in the moonlight, she murmured to me that if we parted, the mountain behind her would disappear; she would turn her head and see nothing but a stretch of open land, desolate and hazy, and she would be like a lonely shadow. I was so moved I couldn't contain myself. A feeling of warm emotion surged through me. I turned around and dived into a nearby bar.

Perhaps there is no hope for me. Perhaps.

I casually strolled out into the street. It was extremely busy, a boundless universe crowded with cars and people. But I felt terribly lonely. I was fretting so much I didn't want to go for a drink; I didn't want to get drunk. I went to watch a film, but, instead of helping shake off this mood, it only added to my gloom. Some underground communists, wearing *qipao* dresses that revealed all their curves and most of their thighs, were desperately on the run. The baddies chasing after them, couldn't catch them even on their motorbikes. Bloody absurd. The baddies, whoever they were, were all men, so of course they couldn't be allowed to catch the women, otherwise the director would have to arrange for them to do things like rip off the women's clothes, a huge offence against decency. To tell the truth, I didn't believe that the slick-haired powder-faced men and women in the film were members of the underground communist organization at all. If they were, then going through fire and water to save people would really be too easy.

II

Back at home, I picked up a collection of poems which the "poet", Present Tense, had sent me a few days earlier. He likes to write his poems in English. I don't know whether he tries to be deliberately obscure or whether he has only limited ability, but he never uses tenses properly, so everyone calls him Present Tense. Whatever the case, he'll probably continue to misuse tenses till the day he dies.

Q read the poems first, and, without pretending to be polite, her verdict was, "A load of rubbish." This collection of poems was, in fact, enough to make you sick, full of lines like "I am so and so", "I'm like so and so", as though if the author didn't exist, then nothing would exist. What are you? You're a ball of shit. What are you like? You're like someone suffering from Ménière's syndrome! I've seen such a case. When you have an attack of this illness, even though you're foaming at the mouth, you still keep screaming and shouting. Perhaps he thinks it's as easy creating beauty in a poem as Dong Shi[1] knitting her brows.

That year, I had only recently left university. I didn't say I graduated, don't get me wrong. Fortunately, my results in nine subjects were all below twenty percent; fortunately, the form I had when I was taking the university entrance exams had completely deserted me; fortunately, I caught a serious illness so that I and the university were able to part in a gentlemanly manner, without embarrassment to anyone.

That year there was a big classical revival in art circles. At the time, people didn't yet think it glorious to discuss Sartre, Freud, etc. In the bookshops, it was still Austen and Chaucer, and in the concert halls it was still Beethoven and the like. Occasionally, I used to go to concerts.

The men were loudly showing off, and the women were being coy. They really looked like models in a fashion parade. The choice of the concert hall grounds as a place for social intercourse before the concert was just right. All the way from the grounds to the concert hall door was the smell of powder and perfume. I dare say that in this group of people, there were only a few who understood music, but they were all putting on an act, posing as lovers of culture. And in order to pose as lovers of culture they only needed to clap enthusiastically at the end. I figured that if I selected any girl from the group and asked her to choose between Beethoven and Shylock, she would definitely and without hesitation choose the latter. If Beethoven had spent his whole life searching for love, even if he had continued searching right up to the present day, he wouldn't have had much hope of finding it. Perhaps it's not only women who are to blame. There's Yin and Yang and the Five Elements, metal, wood, water, fire and earth. If one were missing, we wouldn't have the material world! Likewise, we need all different kinds of people.

---

[1] Dong Shi was reputedly an ugly woman who "knitted her eyebrows" in imitation of the famous beauty, Xi Shi, only to make herself look even uglier.

A European-looking girl, a handkerchief to her nose, was walking back and forth in the crowd, and looking all around, probably in search of someone....

Present Tense happened to be there too, probably to do a bit of socializing. He used to be my classmate at university. Because he had taken exams in philosophy amongst other things, he knew quite a lot about things like dialectics, so he always got excellent marks. His mind was constantly taken up with thoughts of being a postgraduate student. If there was a competition for that, it wouldn't be difficult for this guy to score well.

"What, you're not planning to transfer somewhere else?" That's really bloody wicked and mean. Present Tense had heard that I'd been assigned to work in a restaurant; comparing our situations boosted his sense of superiority. From his tone of voice, it was as if I deserved more sympathy than a political criminal at the time of The Gang of Four. I really did wonder why universities always had rubbish like him in them. It's not surprising that my buddy, whom we called Old Wei, explained why he wanted to go to university in this way: "There are lots of classy girls at university."

"That's right, I don't want to go anywhere else, I just want to carry on filling my belly with offal at the restaurant," I replied, casually. "What about you? How are you getting on?"

"I'm writing a few bits and pieces." Present Tense was perfectly serious, but I could barely stop myself from laughing out loud.

I've read what he's written, and it's all nonsense. Things like "The heroin illusion of life" and "I'm a steamed sponge cake, mixed with cornmeal", are some of the more accurate metaphors he's used. That face of his really looks like a steamed cornmeal bun turned upside down. And there's more, like "A human being is a dish of fried shredded meat and vegies worth twenty-five cents", "Truth, goodness and beauty are chewing gum", and "Real unhappiness is when there is no love", throughout his entire collection of maxims and philosophical theories. Though he's supposed to know everything, I could never work out how people were meant to be fried shredded meat and vegies.

Is it implied meaning? humorous? profound? Bloody absurd! If I had any liking for him at all, I'd teach him how to play poker for money or something, just to stop him from always wasting his time.

The European-looking girl came over; she was with Present Tense. Present Tense quickly left me to one side and started chatting to her. A group of girls had their eyes fixed enviously on them, looking at the girl's buttons, hairstyle, etc.

Physically, Present Tense would never score points. I was much taller and bigger, stronger and healthier, and more handsome. In the past, I loved nothing more than to listen to the sighs of those girls, after their hopes had been dashed, "Oh, I thought you were an artist!" It really made me split my sides laughing. I was extremely pleased with myself. I really liked using the power of this inborn talent to trick those simpering girls in Beijing. It gave me so much pleasure!

The European-looking girl glanced at me in a way that was so familiar. It turned out that even girls not from China are damn well like that too.... Present Tense probably felt insecure, and he quickly whispered something to the girl. The expression on her face was one of incomprehension. I figured that Present Tense may have made a mistake with his tenses again. He gesticulated flatteringly, and the girl began laughing. The group of girls didn't want to be left out of it all, even though they only knew a few letters of the alphabet, and they also began to laugh mockingly, eyeing me at the same time. Present Tense wanted to make use of the small advantage his mistake had brought. But it just so happened that I was in good form, so I roared out: "Hey, you old bastard! Come over here. I should ask you for the money you borrowed to gamble. Come over here!" Present Tense pretended to be deaf and dumb, and quickly went to tip the ash off his cigarette. The fellow is really a joke. Just a minute ago, he was throwing butts all over the floor with me, but now he was running more than twenty metres to the rubbish bin to tip the ash off his cigarette. The European-looking girl had really temporarily civilized him ....

That day was the first time I saw Q. She was wearing a black V-neck blouse with short sleeves and light blue jeans, and her hair was done up in a pony-tail. She was wrapped in body-hugging clothes which showed off her voluptuous curves. That most voluptuous part of her trembled rhythmically in time with the seductive sound of her heels, constantly moving in all directions, as if on elastic. This, together with her flashing eyes, could really make the crowds of men waiting on street corners to pick up an exciting date swoon into raptures.

She didn't have a ticket, and was walking up and down; her elegant legs were just like those of a strong and healthy horse impatiently waiting for a good rider. This was a wonderful opportunity. Present Tense had just given me two tickets; he was able to get hold of such things through his many connections.

I was probably too forward. The heat from my words fell on her face. She watched me closely, her eyes like a big mountain cat's. She took the ticket without saying thanks and, without even paying for it, walked into the theatre.

Needless to say, I stuck close to her. The art college badge on her chest glinted, and distracted me even more. It seemed as though there were some decent girls at university after all; perhaps they turned up after I had left. I don't know whether it was a nerve inside me that was functioning in a strange way, but, although I did my best to look elsewhere, I always ended up looking at her. In the darkness, her two large eyes were fixed on the conductor. To my surprise she didn't look at me, not even a quick glance. Was it because I wasn't someone like Karajan or Ozawa?

I have never been one to pretend; I say whatever I have to say and do whatever I have to do. But those large mountain-cat eyes stopped me from doing anything rash or improper. I even thought about asking for the money for the ticket as a last resort.

"Hey, how about explaining this to me." Finally, I couldn't help holding up the program.

As it happened, the movement in the piece was light-hearted.

Those large mountain-cat eyes stared at me again for a few seconds, making me feel embarrassed. I had a great urge to cover them with my lips.

The interval passed, and when the Debussy piece was about to finish, she suddenly turned around:

"Listen! This gives you the feeling of wanting to take hold of something." Her tone was as cold as the metal rail I was grasping.

That nerve that had been functioning strangely finally relaxed. I no longer needed to look directly at her, and I could discard that last resort that I'd earlier considered. But it was difficult for us to talk. I was like someone striking all sides of a flint to see which side would be able to produce some sparks. I struck the flint till I was exhausted, only to find that there was still nothing.

However, everything that happened later proved that I was right to be so forward at the time.

The concert finished. Several people said hello to her. It seemed as though she knew all the men and women in the world. But, after she finished saying hello, she still remembered to turn and look for me.

"I'm also going in that direction." I had probably lost my way, because, it was exactly the opposite direction I had intended to go....

As we walked along, she smiled occasionally, but remained silent. Her mood was exactly the same as the strong feeling I have today to pour out my heart to someone about my loneliness. I really want to talk with her about those things that one can only reveal to one's intimate friends.

"Let's play a game. Each of us come up with expressions using the word *xiao*, to smile or laugh," she suggested.

"OK! I'll go first," I quickly agreed. "*Daxiao*—laughter", "*lengxiao*—sneer", "*huaixiao*—evil laugh", "*qiexiao*—surreptitious laugh", "*shanxiao*—mock", "*weixiao*—smile", "*jiaxiao*—false laughter", "*chunxiao*—foolish smile", "*chixiao*—mad laughter", "*kuxiao*—bitter laughter", "*yi zhi yan ku, yi zhi yan xiao*—crying on one side, laughing on the other."

"Any more?" She looked pleased with herself. I couldn't think of any more. I felt that the game was rather childish.

"*Pi xiao rou bu xiao*—put on a false smile." Perfectly serious, she added this final summary: "These constitute the entire range of theatrical emotions in life."

Needless to say, I had met up with a female soul-mate. There was some book which said that men shouldn't come into contact with a female soul-mate; countless numbers of heroes and good fellows have come to grief because of it.

Later she proved that she wasn't just playing with me. She was really nice, and not only just in that old bed....

That evening, before I knew her name was Q, we climbed up the Mount Everest of "love" at equal speed.

"I'm called Q," she told me flatly, then said slowly, as she fastened her bra, "It seems as though you can't begin to talk about understanding one another until after you've got to this stage, isn't that right?"

I languidly told her a few things about myself. Luckily, it hadn't crossed her mind that I was an "artist". "People work to make a living. Since whatever you do is to earn money, then you may as well do the easiest work possible!" This sounded a bit like a solemn pledge of love. It might be hard to believe but, when she had finished saying these girlish words, I rolled off the bed and knelt at her feet, tightly clutching her knees. I was so moved that my eyes were brimming with hot tears. Like the Madonna, she stroked me, as though she wanted to give me boundless protection, as though from that time on I would never be hurt again....

I like girls like her who have an artistic imagination and who are wanton, who are mature and yet childish. I even thought about a warm and cosy home that I could return to every night, a little nest, full of atmosphere....

A delicious feast on a wonderful evening, the twinkling lights of countless homes....

A large writing desk, a dark green tablecloth, a large pile of books on the table....

Each of us sitting at opposite ends....

A garden in the moonlight. Grieg, Kafka....

Of course, there is no feast that doesn't come to an end.

Is there anything we can never get enough of? You can get enough of suffering and you can also damn well get enough of happiness!

She forced me to be like her and take up a so-called "career". She said that since there was no virgin land around, I would have to cultivate my own little patch of garden well. It really was a pity that she couldn't recognize that every person has their own place in life. As long as you are willing to work, whatever position it happens to be, no-one can say that you are not pursuing some kind of career....

Also, in another sense, like Q, I was also involved in "art". I'm not talking about the short stories I sometimes write that are unintelligible to others and irrelevant to myself. I'm talking about my job.

Whenever I spread a starched white tablecloth on the table, line up different sized sparkling long-stem glasses, pour different coloured wines, and then wait for customers to arrive, I always proudly admire the masterpieces created by the winemakers. Against the snow-white tablecloth beneath the magnificent large crystal chandelier, the colours of all the different wines glitter, sparkling and translucent. It was said that there was a great oil painter who had searched his whole life for this kind of colour effect, but he died before he could see my wine under the chandelier.

Carrying a stainless steel tray, I walk back and forth on the soft carpet, the reflection from the tray flashing all over the ceiling. At times like this the one-room restaurant is so quiet, and it seems as though this reflection is my good companion, as though it has come to whisper secretly to me so I won't feel lonely. Before the customers arrive, I feel in my heart that life is elegant, magnificent and glorious.

Of course, there is no feast that doesn't come to an end.

Once the customers are seated, before they have even taken up their chopsticks, they almost instantly completely destroy my "art". It's not like the art that Q is engaged in. After one or two hours, her music is still damn well lingering in the roofbeams and everyone forgets to eat meat for three days.

III

I really liked my job; that is to say, in the restaurant where I earned my living, I liked to get on with things, feeling all "keyed up". I was quite willing to let the customers who had come from all over the place order me around. Because of it, I felt the world still needed me a little, that people still needed me a little. Because of it, I felt that perhaps I still was of some value. At the same time, when I put myself in others' hands I felt relaxed. I didn't need to think about what I should do, I didn't need to decide anything. For me, my one day off every week weighed more heavily on me than my work. On each occasion, just before this day arrived, I would imagine a lot of things on my way home after work: for example, how I would climb onto my balcony and count how many cars passed in an hour and what cars they were; or I would go downstairs and count how many windows there were in the building, how many of them were closed, and so on... but everything was always disturbed by Q's resoundingly enterprising spirit. She would throw me into her room, then go off by herself. That's nothing in itself, but what got me was that it disturbed my upbeat mood. How could I possibly study something conscientiously, as she expected? How could I be like her and embrace Debussy, Verdi, and the rest?

I walked into a public phone booth and without thinking dialled G's home. She used to be a fair-weather friend of mine, but I'd heard that she had recently given up drink, and had bought a textbook of Chen Lin's or someone and was learning ABC from the TV at home.

"Hello! Hello!" Still no answer. Best if someone answered quickly, so that I wouldn't have time to get fed up and maybe hang up once I'd thought better of the whole thing.

"Hello...." Good! G must have been studying hard because she already knew how to use her English.

"Hi, let's go and eat!"

"Mm...." The sound was long and drawn out, she was back to the same old ways. "I'm really busy, but...."

"Like hell you're busy!"

"OK, you old dog!"

If there is anything I detest, it's the stuff that women put on their faces. I don't know what it is exactly, but it looks and smells like lime. And it was this smell that she brought along with her.

I didn't say a word, but I felt extremely depressed.

She started to eat, her cheeks bulging as though they had been stuffed with two goose eggs. She also picked her teeth with a red-painted little finger-nail. I couldn't stand it any more, even though it was her treat.

"You are really disgusting."

She stared at me for a few moments, then got up and walked out. With an affected step, her short hair swinging, she probably thought of herself as being free and unrestrained. In the past when we were friends, as soon as I touched upon something she didn't like, she would always get up and walk off, whatever the occasion, leaving me like a fool by myself. Then, just like it's usually written in books, I would angrily walk off too.

I wanted to go and look up Old Wei. I liked Old Wei. He was the only close friend I had during my pitifully brief life at university. There was nothing I couldn't tell him. He was a quiet sort of person, who never said a word. I liked the expression in his eyes, like a dog holding back the impulse to bite someone and run away. In that seven-storey block of flats, I had the good fortune to share Room 707 with Old Wei, one on the upper bunk, one on the lower. I couldn't get to sleep, and kept tossing and turning, thinking that this would definitely disturb him. But surprisingly, I couldn't even hear the sound of his breathing. I was afraid he might have suddenly come down with some serious illness, and I climbed the side of the bed to have a look. In the moonlight, his eyes blazed with a fierce light. I was so frightened I hurriedly covered my head with the quilt.

Of all the people in my dormitory, only he really kept to himself. When we started living together, all the others apart from myself were aloof and standoffish, as though everyone else had the plague. No-one took the initiative to get close to anyone else. But after only a few days, because everyone had started getting too close, for example, someone used someone else's washbowl, someone drank the water that someone else had boiled, someone used someone else's brush on their own shoes, arguments constantly flared up. Only Old Wei remained aloof and out of it all.

The people who were at high school when the Cultural Revolution started are really different from us. I think that we were right in the middle of two generations of people, the ancients and the newcomers. To me, Old Wei really was an ancient. He had experienced all the hardships of life, and had been to places like Heilongjiang, Guangdong, Shanxi.... Once, he told me that he had read most of Balzac before he was ten, and in one month had memorized a thousand English words. When I was ten, the extent of my knowledge of foreign places was that damn Albanian film *Storm off the Coast.* He showed me his first year textbook, which was full of

"In the spring of the fourth year of the reign of Emperor Song Renzong,[2] Teng Zijing was demoted to the position of head official of Baling prefecture", and suchlike. I remembered my own first year textbook, which was all about "Criticize Lin Biao, Criticize Confucius", and the struggle between Confucianism and Legalism! Old Wei told me about all the "idlers" and "street fighters" of the old days. They always supplied their names first before a fight; it was a time when you couldn't attempt to defeat a man until you knew his name. It only needed one of them to admit defeat, and the other would immediately stop fighting. Then they would have a drink together. But we "street fighters", used large pieces of wood and bricks, and we risked killing people by bashing them over the back of the head, and running off. It seems we really are different; it's just that some older people can't distinguish between us, and lump us all together as one generation.

Some say that the experiences a person has when young can influence the rest of their life. Old Wei probably only had wonderful experiences when he was young, so his results were always among the best in the whole department.

I hurried along towards a place which wound round and round but was called Straight as a Ramrod Lane and found the large compound I was looking for. As soon as I walked through the gate I saw a tap with a rubber pipe over it; an old hunchback was wiping his back with a towel that was so dirty you couldn't tell what colour it was, splashing water everywhere as he did so. Young children crying and shouting, adults affectionately cursing and the sound of a fiddle, sad enough to pull at your heart strings, all combined to form a large and lively chorus. Although the compound was big, squeezed into it were all kinds of little kitchens, making it appear extremely crowded. A small path which encircled these little houses put forth little fingers to each household, so that whichever house you wanted to go to from the compound gate you had to walk on this maze-like path. Often, a man wearing nothing but undershorts and waving a huge cattail leaf fan would walk past, the backs of his shoes trodden down, or a woman, wearing no more on top than a singlet, would

---

[2] That is, 1044.

walk to the tap to throw away some dirty water. Brightly coloured fashionable clothes were drying on an iron wire, and water from the clothes dripped down onto a row of old chamber pots, now used as plant pots, from which grew little flowers and plants that even a botanist might not necessarily be able to name. They were growing quite luxuriantly too....

I made my way to the door of the place where Old Wei lived. The windows of his room were pasted over with issues of *Reference News*. I knocked on the door.

"Who is it?" Muffled sounds came from within. I waited for ages, and finally the door was opened. I was taken aback: it wasn't Old Wei who had come to open the door, but someone else from Room 707, a weird bloke called Puppet Regime.

As soon as I walked in, I saw a young girl straightening her clothes and making a show of sitting properly.

"How's Q?" he quickly put in first.

"Still alive." I felt terribly disappointed.

Puppet Regime was another major reason for my leaving university. At the time I was somewhat extreme, considering it beneath me to mix with such people.

Puppet Regime had the best background in our little group. It was said that his grandfather had kept his pigtail while studying in Germany. Normally, when one talks about "attaching oneself to someone or something", it probably refers to attaching oneself to men of high culture, but he attached himself to hooligans. It was said that he led a pretty dissolute life, which led me to think that there must have been girls out there who didn't like strong rippling muscles beneath bronzed, glistening skin but who did admire legs as thin as the hemp sticks for beating down ripe apricots and dates.... If you fancied flattering him a little, he would immediately become extremely coarse and think it was great. On his left eyelid he had a scar. If eight hours of every day were set aside for grooming purposes, he would spend seven and a half of them looking in the mirror. The time left over would be spent "partly on religious cultivation of the self and partly on being a Confucian gentleman"— that is, half the time would be spent brushing his hair and washing his face, and the other half on silently feeling sorry about his scar.

Then, he would fly off to his lectures like a comet. It was rumoured that he once boldly confessed his feelings of love to a student. She tactfully rejected him, but he just wouldn't let the matter drop and kept asking her why. In the end she was forced to tell him the truth.... "For no other reason than that golden line on your eyelid!" Thereupon, everyone started calling him Golden Line—Puppet Regime, and then to make it easier to say, it was shortened to Puppet Regime.[3]

"He writes novels." This was how he unexpectedly introduced me to the girl in the room, who looked about twenty years old.

"Oh, is that right?" More simpering. Even Q is better than that, because although she prettifies herself with make-up, she doesn't put on an affected manner.

"I don't write novels, I work in a restaurant." I had no intention whatsoever of putting Puppet Regime in a good light. I was pondering why Old Wei should lend the room to him.

The expression on the girl's face began to change. "This is my wife." Puppet Regime pointed to her. I almost vomited. She was probably the kind of lascivious woman experiencing the "pain of having no love" as described in the novels written by Present Tense.

"Do you write love stories?" The girl emitted a cat-like squeal.

"I often write about fights between myself and my wife, about nibbling on pigs' tails, eating donkeys' hooves, and the like."

Her eyes rolled upwards and she put on a show of watching me with profound interest as though she regretted not being able to stuff her long eyelashes into my eyes.

"Let's play chess," I said to Puppet Regime. "I came to look for Old Wei to have a couple of games with him."

"Old Wei has rented the room to me at 35 *yuan* a month."

"Oh!" I was thinking how good Old Wei was at making money.

"Actually 35 *yuan* to buy a month of loose living isn't expensive."

---

[3] The girl referred to the scar as *jin bian*, a homonym for the Chinese characters for Phnom Penh, where there was installed what the Chinese government considered to be a puppet regime.

He took out the chess, though I could see he was rather reluctant. I chose black, because I liked this murderous colour.

"Your go." I was reflecting that this would be a match not played by the rules, because I was going to attack so fiercely he would forget that his horse should move forward and his elephant should move diagonally.

"Canon goes to the middle!" So damn conventional, just like the novels Present Tense writes.

I moved my general back one....

Before taking one of his pieces, I always pointed out his precarious situation so that he could save his game, but he still lost resoundingly. His face began to redden and he insisted on going all out to beat me. I was getting bored with winning, and I wanted to stop playing, but it was going to be difficult for me to get away unless he won a game in front of his wife.

"There are a couple of mates who've invited me out for a drink this evening," he said in an exaggerated manner, his thumb darting upwards. This movement and tone of voice, coupled with his fine glasses, which, rumour had it, his father had brought back from a business trip overseas, made him look like a cartoon character. It was a not particularly ingenious hint for me to leave. I understood what he was getting at but pretended not to.

"Have they invited you out for a soft drink?"

"Come off it, for alcohol!" Terrible. This guy really lacks a sense of humour.

"I'll join you for a couple of glasses!"

"You don't know any of the fellows."

"Perhaps, but I always know a drink." This time he finally understood, and his face went alternately green and white. I really wanted to go and see his mates, but, because I still had Q on my mind, I bade him farewell.

IV

I walked out into the street again. I looked here and there, in shop windows, in bookshop windows. It was only five o'clock. At this time of the day I was at the height of my boredom; if it wasn't a rest day, then it was the busiest and most crowded time on the buses. I only hoped that today would be over quickly; I really was fed up with today.

So, I went into a little bar, bought a plate of peanuts and half a *jin* of spirits and sat down.

A young couple, holding hands, were slurping noodles, busily chatting as they ate.

"Have you read Skiski's book?"[4] A question sweetly asked.

"What?" A muffled reply.

"You should love me just like that."

"I'm damn well good enough to you already. I've borrowed so much money to buy you so many things, my mom almost killed me."

I felt sick. I poured my drink into the ashtray, then stubbed my cigarette in it. I walked out without getting back the fifty-cent deposit on the patterned porcelain bowl which contained my drink.

I walked as far as the concert hall and sat down on the steps, absent-mindedly watching people pass by. I wondered if I was one of those individuals who had no future. I thought about what else I should want, apart from my job. What else should I want? And who should I want it from?

Q once told me that she divided people into four categories: those who were clever and good, those who were clever and bad, those who were stupid and good, those who were stupid and bad.

"You're a head which doesn't have solid shoulders for a woman to rest her weary self upon." Q once used this line from a poem to make fun of me.

"I'm hoping that I can rest in a woman's gentleness for the rest of my life. My head may not be weary but everything else is."

"Women are even more weary." Perhaps what Q said was right, but I wasn't willing to acknowledge it. Maybe she could see into my heart. I don't know why she finished with this sentence: "You are a clever, bad person."

---

[4] An invention of the author.

Once, Q arranged for me to see some performance with her. As a result of this incident, which had nothing to do with us, I classified her, according to her own method of classification.

At the theatre door, we saw a young fellow, dressed in grease-stained workclothes carefully caressing with his dirty carrot-thick fingers a ticket bought at an inflated price. I knew a lot of singers, dancers and actors, and upon reflection, I could see that Q by comparison measured up well. They looked down on fellows like that, but they would still cheat someone like him out of money he had earned through blood and sweat. Don't be taken in by their singing and dancing, bowing to the left and saluting to the right, as though everyone in the audience was their seventy- or eighty-year-old grandfather. In fact, all they want deep down is that the audience should disperse as quickly as possible so that they can share out the profits faster. I heard that there was some actress who called out on stage "Do you want to kiss me?" or something. That young fellow we had seen at the theatre door would have gone up to nibble her beautiful cheeks. Then, having whistled and jeered no less than the others in the audience, he would have felt quite content and, the next day, gone off to weld steel doors or whatever.

On that evening it was a celebrity concert. The way the orchestra had been arranged looked just like the way the good fellows from Liang Shan Po used to sit,[5] as they drank wine from huge bowls and divided up and weighed the gold on great scales. In the back row, I noticed a woman on strings who looked like Q but who played with enormous effort, which saddened me greatly. I pointed her out to Q, who looked dejected. It probably made her think of her own fate....

This evening, it was a world-class string performance. Q would come. There was no way she would miss this opportunity.

Perhaps I really love her. Does she also love me? Perhaps!

She arrived, with some bread and sausages, as though nothing had happened. I really didn't like watching the violinist on stage dragging her bow back and forth as though she were mopping the

---

[5] From the Ming dynasty (1368-1644) novel *Shuihu zhuan* (Outlaws of the Marsh).

floor, and with so much vigour that her face was covered in sweat, only I didn't dare say.

After the performance, we left the concert hall. I offered Q my arm, like I had done so many times in the past once we had made up after a quarrel. But she deliberately ignored me, and rebuked me by saying, "You don't do anything."

But I knew that she wanted to be a bit gentler.

"I'm writing!"

"Like hell you're writing."

"You don't understand." I smiled and told her for the first time about my unique writing technique. "Every day I think of something and write it down. There is no theme and no coherence. When I have written a whole lot of pages, I just put them together and, hey presto, it's done. It's called a pack-of-cards novel. It's just like life. You can look at it however you want, but you can't explain it."

She smiled. In high spirits, I told her that I had been to see a film to release some of my feelings of frustration. But I didn't dare tell her that in my boredom I had gone to play chess, and even less did I dare mention that G had invited me to dinner.

V

It seemed as though Q wouldn't let be until she had dragged me up to a certain level; she was determined to turn me into someone like all the others, what I mean is, all those pursuing a "career". All those who dress tastefully, whose manner is not at all vulgar, whose speaking is refined, who wear glasses, or whatever. However that may be, it wasn't that I didn't understand what was involved in the work such people do, but I just wasn't interested in any of it. You could say that I didn't like anything I understood....

I thought of Present Tense, Puppet Regime and the other students from Room 707. When you asked them why they were studying, not one of them could give a reason. They didn't even say it was for the revolution or whatever. Only Old Wei was different. One day he finally let me into his secret.

"I study as though there is no tomorrow, and I do it so that more people will understand and need me." That was why I liked Old

Wei. If he didn't say anything, then he didn't say anything. When he did say something, he said it honestly. As for the others, whenever I think of them, I never feel the slightest regret that I left university because of my "illness". They were always immaculately dressed, quite striking in appearance. But when Present Tense used to take off his shoes, which were so shiny you could see your reflection in them, everyone in the dormitory would get ready to flee, because he never washed his feet.

Did Q really want me to be like them?

"Your attitude to life is on the downslide," Q once said to me. I didn't really agree with this conclusion of hers. I thought that I looked as if I was gently and slowly drifting downwards, but in my soul there was something rising, sublime. There are many things in life which can inspire me. For instance, at dusk when I am at the foot of the mountain range on the outskirts of the city looking at the cluster of mountains, as if guessing a riddle, I imagine what there is by the furthest mountain, with curling wisps of sunset cloud and the fading sun snuggling close to it. Is it the sea? Is it grasslands? Is it an apricot grove?...

"What is there over by that mountain?"

One day I asked Q, and she gave a very prosaic answer: "Over by that mountain are more mountains!" Perhaps she was right, but I didn't want to believe it. What there was over by that mountain continued to inspire me, even though the answer she gave was incised deeply into my brain....

"But, once there is a mountain, there will be people who climb it," I said.

It's just the same as if you do something for someone, and they are sincerely thankful. Such things I like, such things inspire me.

To help my writing along, Q introduced me to a lot of eminent people, most of whom were well-known and middle-aged.

"If you're writing stories, you cultivate a small circle of acquaintances," she said. "Everyone can read one another's work, and so make speedy progress."

"Writing stories is like this...." The opening remarks of these famous people went on forever.

"Mmm." Usually I made no comment.

"How old are you?"

"Twenty."

"Where do you work?"

"At XX Restaurant." The whole thing was like an oral version of my residence booklet.

"Is that so?" The most marvellous moment had arrived. Their little opaque cross-eyes, which only famous people have, would light up. When the conversation got to this point it took a familiar turn.

"Last time we ate out, we had to queue up for a whole morning. Next time, we'll come to look for you and we won't have so much trouble."

"Next time I'll help out." I put up with the damn humiliation.

"Waiter, I've invited a few foreigners along. Can you give us some special consideration?"

"Foreigners? Even Martians have to damn well wait in line like everyone else!"

I began to run back and forth between these people. Actually, at twenty years of age I was already mature, and I had also spent time wandering far and wide twelve years prior to that, so such small things shouldn't have bothered me. But sometimes an indulgent fantasy of trusting to luck overwhelmed me. Just the same as if, for instance, you have wandered into Zhangjiakou in the small hours of a December morning. It is one of those nights when the cold wind rips a person to shreds. You are waiting, waiting for a train that is heading towards warmth. To warm your ears you cover them with your hands, then you blow warm air onto your hands. Finally you pick up a straw rope and tie it around your waist and begin to run for all you are worth along the platform. When you discover that all of this is useless and the train isn't coming, you—ah! I bet that at that time, you won't think of a warm fire, or that single bed at home with the golden brown woollen blanket. Trusting to luck, you just want to cry. You will think—go on and cry! If you have a good cry then perhaps the wind will stop blowing and the train will come. So you open your mouth wide and wail at the pork-liver coloured night sky.

"A person without an objective has no worth." I have pondered over this sentence by Feuerbach ever since reading it as a young boy. Stories—are they my objective?

VI

Q and I finally separated.

After that time we had made up after a quarrel, there was a period when Q wasn't always so hypercritical of me. We both did our best to avoid sensitive questions, and we were at peace with each other. But she did impose a few conditions. I wasn't, for instance, to interfere with her violin practice.

In order to fit in with me, she compressed perhaps a week's work into three days, so we always met three or four times a week, and would go off for a drink or whatever. She asked that each time we got together, I should tell her something. For example, the last time we met just before our separation, I told her the story of *The Counterfeiter*, of how old Profitendieu read his mother's love letters on the sly, only to find that he was illegitimate, how he left in anger, leaving behind a malicious letter for his stepfather, etc. etc.[6]

I don't really want to know why we split up, but I do know. It was a Wednesday, midday, when I got a phone call from her.

"Hello, I've got some good news for you."

"It's been a while since I've had any good news."

"There's a college that's enrolling new students and its special discipline is just right for you...."

Had the curtain on war been opened again? This time, it was she who had started it.

I controlled my anger, and remained silent for a while. She was waiting on her side of the phone....

"What I say is... you may as well just leave me. Really, Q, let's just forget it!"

Silence.

"Was there anything else? I'm really busy right now."

---

[6] The character referred to is Bernard Profitendieu in the novel *The Counterfeiters* (Les Faux-monnayeurs, 1925) by André Gide.

"Wait for me at the usual place tonight!" She was tense and viciously swore at me before slamming down the phone.

After work, I walked haltingly towards the old destination—the place where we had first met. It wasn't that I was tired, I was just absentmindedly thinking my own thoughts, colourful thoughts that appeared one after another. I was looking, but not really seeing anything, listening, but not really hearing anything, listless, as though in a dream. Bus drivers were hooting their horns for all they were worth, and the bells of bicycles joined in the chorus. Policemen in their police boxes at the crossroads were surrounded by a swirling chaos. People eating ice-lollies were carrying all kinds of bags on their backs and in their hands. No-one else it seemed was like me, stupidly grinning, casually glancing here and there, empty-headed.

Around five o'clock the sun was still shining, and I squinted to look at Q who was waiting for me opposite, next to the telephone booth. She was wearing a sleeveless dress, her arms softly rounded. I really found her very attractive....

"Have you got a death wish?" A bus suddenly braked about two metres from me. The sound was damn unpleasant. The driver slammed the door of his bus shut and strode over to me. Immediately, a group of people gathered around to watch.

Sometimes you just can't explain why your heart feels glad. Sometimes you are not thinking of anything, then in a blinding flash you recall all these impressions without time or space, and then perhaps a stupid grin appears on your face.

"I'm talking to you! Did you hear me?"

"You're talking to me?"

The people around broke into guffaws of laughter.

"Are you damn crazy?"

"Yes I am. Just this morning I escaped over the wall of an asylum. The doctors chased me for 700 *li*...." I whispered, hand cupped around my mouth and his ear. I peered around mysteriously.

The driver looked at me suspiciously and took a step back. A policeman ran over. The number of onlookers was increasing. I felt very pleased with myself: Q, Q, here I am, the centre of attention. How come you can't see me?

I stood on tiptoe and smiled and waved at her. This time you have to forgive me. I haven't deliberately arrived late. There was nothing I could do about it.

Everyone looked across the road. Finally, Q saw me and hurriedly ran across, not forgetting to use the pedestrian crossing. The wind blew her brown dress tight across her body. My dearest!

"The fellow's got no brains."

"That was really dangerous!"

Those who had come to watch the excitement were chattering away. Bloody annoying! It's said that the Japanese never stand around gawping on the street. They are all too busy bustling about. No wonder they are all so rich.

Q looked me up and down, ascertained I was still in one piece, then quickly apologized to the driver. Q was really great! Her manner was just right, not too humble, and not too arrogant. The driver must have succumbed to her charms because he left me there and went back to his bus, taking his anger out on his 50-decibel horn instead. Thereupon the crowd scattered.

The policeman brought us to his traffic box and reprimanded Q, implying that people like me should always have someone accompanying them when crossing the road. Q must have nodded her head several times. I was thinking about her coming across the road just now, with those beautiful strides I found so seductive. Finally, I thought I heard the policeman asking what relationship existed between us.

"I'm her uncle," I broke in quickly. Q stared at me in surprise and then pulled me away. This time she took me across the pedestrian crossing.

After crossing the road, Q asked me why I said I was her uncle, and not her nephew. I really couldn't say. She remained silent after that.

Suddenly, she gave a sob, turned back and went into a little garden at the side of the road. I walked over and sat beside her, then came out with my usual predictable tomfoolery.

"Come with me to the mental hospital. I want to be examined."

She said nothing.

"It would be really great to go there. I wouldn't have to be responsible for anything. Apart from listening to bells ringing and eating my meals, the whole day I could just sit in the sunshine foolishly rubbing my belly."

"You're so damn silly. Skip all that rubbish, OK?" In the end, she couldn't hold back a giggle.

Oh! Q! We are in fact all children, yes! We are all nature's children, whether we are professors, heads of departments, or whatever. And nature gives me sunshine, air and water in the same way it gives them to everyone else. Why do you want to try and make me do something I can't do or don't want to do?

"All right." I pretended to be serious. "Tell me your plans."

I have to say that she declared war on me again, going on about "you need to be more realistic", "you have to think more of yourself", "you need to make plans for yourself". Is it really possible that if this ordinary life of mine, so similar to that of millions of others, carries on in this way, it's going to end up a disaster? So, I agreed to put my name down for the entrance exams, though I was afraid that the whole thing was just an illusion....

VII

Several days passed and there I was sitting in a large classroom in XX College taking the exam....

I stared blankly at the questions on the exam paper, which seemed of no particular relevance to me. I don't know why I felt not the slightest bit of self-confidence and had none of the competitive spirit that I had had a few years previously when taking my university entrance exams.

What was "thinking in terms of images"?

Othello performing a section of Peking opera, adopting the gait of a hammer-wielding general; old Master Gao, a skull cap on his head, performing a ballet lift; and Xianglin Sao's scissor jumps. Anything that entailed this kind of creative mental activity could be called "thinking in terms of images".

Of course, I couldn't answer in that way. Well, how else could I answer? I thought of God. I thought, if, at a crucial time like this, he wasn't prepared to extend his plump, kindly hand to help me, then he must be planning on some day preventing me from jumping to my death from a high building.

He's always more of a damn hindrance than a help!

That Short Blue Chinese Jacket who had come to sign up for the entrance exams at the same time as me was now sitting not far in front of me, wholly absorbed in his writing. He'll definitely be answering the questions well. I hoped he knew what "thinking in terms of images" was. I hoped he knew everything and could write it all down in his answers. It looked as though he had a fair amount of competitive spirit, and was full of confidence. I sincerely hoped he would do well in his exam, do well enough to pass, and become another example of a member of a 10,000 *yuan* household getting to university, even though he wouldn't necessarily learn very much....

I was bent over my desk, dozing, sleepy, as I had been the whole summer. But I still had to rack my brains, for love, and in order unfortunately to fulfil Q's expectations of me.

On the day when Q came with me to sign up for the entrance exams, the sun was shining brightly. The large teaching block of XX College looked really beautiful, with lush green Boston ivy climbing right up to the roof.

"You see, if you receive a few years of systematic education here, you'll be able to achieve something." Q seemed to have every faith in my worth, but she didn't realize that there was no way my worth could find expression at university.

The two lecturers in the enrolment office were sitting with their backs to an open window, a mug of tea in front of each of them.

"From out of town?" One of them languidly took a sip of tea and then politely put this question to Short Blue Chinese Jacket.

"Uh huh." He nodded awkwardly.

Short Blue Chinese Jacket was carrying a satchel on which a few lotus flowers had been clumsily sewn by some village girl. Across his chest was slung an army canteen, his trouser bottoms were short and skimpy, and on his feet, he was wearing a pair of plastic sandals.

"Have you just come off the train?"

"Uh huh."

"You've come a long way. Have a drink of water!" For some reason, the lecturer intentionally winked at his companion, at the same time gesturing dramatically towards the hot water container.

Q must have understood the lecturer's sense of humour. "You see, that's your competitor."

"Perhaps there's some girl who has great expectations of him, just as you have of me."

I wasn't too pleased. Did the people from Room 707 act in such a contemptible manner just to feel superior to Short Blue Chinese Jacket? Was Q's incessant nagging only so that I wouldn't be "reduced" to becoming "common" like Short Blue Chinese Jacket?

I like Old Wei.

It came to my turn.

"And your record of formal schooling?"

Where was I going to get a record of formal schooling from?

But nothing presented difficulties for Q. On the last day of exam registration, she found it, although it was only a record of my senior middle school education, and didn't mention the fact that I had been to university.

"Please put your satchel under your chair. If you turn around, we'll take it that you are cheating." The invigilating lecturer was very polite and said this as though he were joking.

The lecturers were all extremely polite, a reflection of their education.

What is dialectics?

I began to arbitrarily put down my views on the exam paper, but I would be damn surprised if the lecturer would be able to appreciate them.

But from the very beginning one had to follow the set rules.

Dialectics is a method for people to understand the world....

Dialectical materialism maintains that....

It was probably the last day of registration, so the second time I came to register for the exam, there was hardly anyone around. The two lecturers were still in front of the window, each with a mug of tea as before.

I leaned against a big tree and took in a deep breath. What force had spurred me on to come twice to this place to register!

76 • Variations Without a Theme

The two lecturers in front of the window looked a little bored. A fly flew back and forth and finally, after going through a process of selection, landed on the nose of one of them, but he was too lazy to brush it away with his hand and, instead, stuck out his tongue to lick it, just like a damn ox.

The other lecturer thought of an absolutely great way of whiling away the time. He randomly pulled out one sheet from a pile of registration forms, looked at it carefully, and then suddenly burst out laughing. He put on a Henan accent that sounded quite authentic, worthy of a graduate from an arts college. Name—XX, studied at XX Commune Middle School, XX county, Henan province, between dates XX and XX. Special achievements: I wrote a novel of 400,000 characters. At this point he other lecturer also burst out laughing.

I was shocked, and felt dizzy. Would this fellow some day out of boredom take out my registration form and have a good laugh at it? Would those twenty years of life in which I had had my fill of bitter experiences also be looked upon by him as worthless? And if I passed the exam, would he sanctimoniously lecture me in the classroom on socialist spiritual civilization?

Q! I only want to be an ordinary man. I've never had the slightest inclination to be a scholar, and now I want to be one even less. Shouldn't I have the right to choose my own path in life and keep my own individuality?

If the person who had been the butt of the lecturer's jokes had personally witnessed the scene just then, what would he have thought? That young fellow from XX commune, XX county, Henan province. Perhaps he wouldn't be too upset over it, but, then again, perhaps it would suddenly shatter that feeling of self-confidence that had sustained him as he travelled from afar to take the exam....

I finally wrote my answer to the question about dialectics, incisively and vividly giving free rein to my thoughts. I want to tell you how I answered: you should look at a person from a dialectical perspective. For example, a particular lecturer is an out-and-out bastard, who likes to help pretty female students catch up with their lessons on a one-to-one basis. He regards peasants, workers and soldiers as common. But you can't simply say that he is a bastard. You have to look at it from a dialectical perspective.

VIII

On a rainy day, following the publication of the names of the successful candidates, I and Q went to visit one of her friends, a woman who was said to be very talented. She could turn stone to gold; after she had polished it, a third year primary student's poetic composition managed to get published and brought in royalties. A while ago, when I was anxiously waiting to pay off drinking debts, I sent her a story I'd written.

From what I could see, she was adept at lying, her manner of speaking was ten times more impressive than her actual ability. She always tried to play each person like a card, though she found me a somewhat thorny card to play. If I was going to do the same to her, what would it be like? If I played "knock on three houses", then she would be the unfortunate three of clubs; if I played "pigs dig the earth", then she would be the losing ace of spades. However, it's very rare that I play poker.

You can understand it when certain people tell lies, one example being the little boy who cried "wolf". With only some big bare mountains around him, and a flock of sheep with their heads down eating grass, it must have been really lonely, so it's no wonder he looked for some way to amuse himself. Another example is Wang Erxiao, who pretended to lead the Japanese straight to the Eighth Route Army so that they could attack it, but instead, the Japanese found themselves encircled by the Eighth Route Army. That kind of lie is also right since it's for the good of the revolution. But this spinster who is more than thirty tells lies out of vanity.

It's not really damn worth telling lies simply for the sake of vanity. Perhaps that's just her nature, but a grown woman of more than thirty should be able to restrain herself. In the past, she had said of herself that she was "a person who had been made abnormal by society".

I think that she lies purely because she thinks there is no-one cleverer than her. She really can't be believed. For example, she would say that today she fell over and found 700 *yuan* on the ground so she'd invite you for a meal. Without any hesitation, I would choose Minim's restaurant.[7] I would also pretend to be extremely envious, just like the prefectural governor of Jiangnan in the home of the Head of Public Works, Li Shen.[8]

You probably can't say that she's a frivolous or flighty woman, it's just that she is used to simpering in front of members of the opposite sex. Luckily, she still wears her hair shoulder-length, a style favoured by young girls, so when she starts simpering, she only makes people's hair stand on end a little, and she doesn't go so far as to frighten people to death.

She has a fox's face and sallow skin. What is strange is that in her room she has hanging miniature reproductions of paintings, foreign dolls, photos of the Japanese film star Takakura Ken, and so on. You expect the seven dwarfs to appear at any moment

When Q and I got to her place, she was crazily drawing something on a piece of paper, a cigarette hanging out of the corner of her mouth. She was wearing masses of cheap jewellery on her hands and around her neck.

"I've come to fetch the story I wrote." Q was still exchanging polite greetings with her, but I came straight to the point.

"Oh! Was it you who wrote that piece, 'A Story of Water, Rain and Thunder'?" she said as she rooted about in a basket that looked as though it was for holding cabbage, but in which was a jumble of fashion pictorials, fruit and a half-knitted sweater.

"What I wrote was the story of Caesar and Pan Jinlian."

"Really!" She looked up at me. "I'll have another look for it." As she rooted around, she prattled on, I don't know what about, with a cute expression on her face.

"Your novel wasn't bad. I gave it to XX to have a look at." Another famous person.

---

[7] A pun on the restaurant name, Maxims.

[8] The author is referring to an incident during the Tang dynasty (618-907) when the famous poet and senior minister, Li Shen, invited Liu Yuxi, previously a prefectural governor, to a sumptious banquet, at which Liu reputedly put on a great show of envying Li's status and wealth.

Whenever she spoke of anyone famous, she always called them by their first name and left out their surname. There was also one category of individuals whom she divided into two groups depending on how famous the individuals were. One lot she called XX the Old and the other Old XX, as though these people were all members of her own clan.

"Oh! That's right! How about buying me two cartons of cigarettes?"

"Pah! I'll damn well buy you two ropes to hang yourself."

I kicked open the door and came out. The sky had darkened, and as I looked at the stars I let out a deep breath, then spat out from deep inside that gutful of cabbage smell.

Damn!

Q came chasing after me. We went off together for dinner. She didn't say anything, and I had a sense that something would definitely happen between us.

We silently sat at a table near the window on the ground floor of XX restaurant. The curtains were half-drawn. Large raindrops pattered on the glass and then slowly slithered down. The street lamps were dim. Q pressed her face close to the window and stared outside.

I couldn't fathom her expression. She lightly twirled around her long-stem glass full of fragrant Wei Mei Si wine. I watched her closely, not knowing what to say.

Q continued to stare outside. I shook the wine bottle in front of her. She waved her hand in refusal and carried on looking outside. I took her glass, meaning to fill it, when she suddenly turned around, snatched the bottle and, holding it around the neck, brought it down ferociously onto the table. She held her head in her hand, her jet-black hair cascading down. I tapped her with my foot and, as if just waking from a dream, she looked around, and then smiled serenely at me.

"Q, one day, I'll make you proud of me."

"Oh, I already feel proud enough."

I started to tell her about *The Counterfeiters*, and about old Profitendieu, even though she probably wasn't listening....

When we left the restaurant, it was already after 10 p.m. We staggered along the muddy road towards the bus stop. Q was silent, indifferently looking at the road, on which scarcely a soul was to be seen. The bus arrived. She jumped on and, now above me, I could see her leaning out of the window, tears streaming down her face....

We separated.

I felt tired and wanted to go home. I thought of how my mom, in order to put clean sheets on my bed, would surely have taken all the books that were thrown in a mess all over the bed and put them back in my bookcase. Today, I'm going to take *The Counterfeiters* out of the bookcase again and continue reading it....

Q, I'm also going to write a story for you. In many years time, when you have been assigned to play the violin with some group, to play for famous decadent singers from some place in Hong Kong, and when after work, on the way home you buy fifty cents' worth of mince and a couple of carrots, I'll still be the same as I am now, without rhyme or reason always happy and absent-minded. And when I cross the road, I'll never look to see whether or not I'm on the pedestrian crossing....

Story of a City

Dedicated to that friend far away who used to say, "If you do nothing, you're on the wrong road, and if you do something, damn it, you're also on the wrong road."

You just wouldn't believe what my wife is like.

If you really want to know all about it, I must start from the beginning.

Of course, I don't need to mention how, so many years ago, she used to wear a little pair of pants that barely covered her bottom, and a small short-sleeve top. As we ran and jumped all over the place, she would hold in one hand a copy of the pictorial, *Little Friends*, and in the other, a marble with a red centre, that I had given her.

I also don't need to tell how at that time I used to risk all my six years of life fighting with other big children from the courtyard who wanted to take her catapult which was made with a rubber band; how she ran back home to tell what was happening, and how my older brother took up of a huge wooden stick taller than a man to come and save my life.

There's no need to tell of any of these things.

There's also how we got all dressed up and went with the grown-ups to a dance held at the office section hall; how she sat on the sofa, her small feet not touching the ground, and how she wailed and sobbed because she couldn't find her mother in the swirling crowd of dancers; how I, to stop her crying, took the opportunity, whilst uncles and aunts were all dancing in a misty haze, to steal some apples from the table.

There's no need to mention any of these things. Since you know of our childhood games, there's no need to mention any of them.

Well, where should I begin, then?

Perhaps I should begin with the pretences, the artificial behaviour between husband and wife that every family experiences; something extremely secret, that you mustn't allow any outsider to see through or understand. There is probably no need to mention this either, since every couple will know what I'm talking about.

To be honest with you, the instant I had the strange idea that I wanted to find a wife, the first girl who came into my crazy mind was her.

Later, she did finally become my wife.

Before we married, on several occasions we recalled old times together as we cuddled on fine spring days under a large cassia tree that stood in front of the grotesque building in which she lived. I discovered that in spirit she had become my wife a million years ago. We had gone through the cretaceous era; through the endless battles of the Spring and Autumn and the Warring States periods; through the Tang dynasty that had nurtured poets; through the Qing dynasty and its long pigtails, the tips of which we can still see to the present day; we had gone through all the countless years of history, and in the end she was still my wife.

I returned to her in this way, bringing a bellyful of painful contradictions that could be used to write more than a hundred versions of the *Record of the Enlightenment of Materialists*,[1] bringing my shadow, and bringing in my wake four or five creditors, both men and women, who were demanding the money I owed them for drink. Of course, all of this was far and long removed from the time of the marble with the red centre, and since then I had undiscerningly experienced many things. It is said that you should be able to differentiate between things, for example, the age at which you begin to learn and understand, the age at which you marry, the age at which you pass the imperial examinations. All these need differentiating. But I don't know why I just never see things as being different. So I've become a freak. But I also don't know how I became a freak, since everyone says that freaks only exist among foreigners.

---

[1] The title is an invention of the author.

On that day, like a cornered animal, I brought to her several men and women creditors who were demanding the money I owed them for drink. If I didn't repay them in full, they threatened to tip out of me all the drink I had imbibed over the past ninety-nine years. I reckoned that if there was someone on this earth who would still extend the hand of friendship to me, it would be her.

"Hi! If you see anyone here you like the look of, help me get rid of one or two."

She looked at me, then at that bunch of people. Then, she wheeled out her bicycle and went to the bank to get some money. Out of the blue, from a sense of pity, they decided to chat with me about something other than money.

"Hey! That girl's really pretty. Who is she?"

"F... you! When you get your money, you can piss off. Why are you asking so many questions?"

They shut up, because if they got in a fight with me, I would naturally no longer need to pay the money I owed them for drink. They could, perhaps, have had the satisfaction of beating me on the belly like a drum, until they had beaten it to pulp. I haven't had a good belly laugh for years. But according to the unwritten rule of buddies, at least a few of the creditors needed to be paid off. They still loved money more.

She came back with the cash. She must have liked the look of every single one of the creditors, because, right in front of me, she distributed uneven wads of notes to each of them. My stomach contracted tightly, and I twitched. In my twenty years of life, I had never experienced a scene more shameful than this. I seemed to see a whole array of things that were good to eat, good to drink, good fun and good to look at, grow wings, and, like a flock of doves, take flight.

"Remember, that's 250 *yuan* altogether." She said to me after the group had moved off.

"I will, I'll remember to my grave."

As I looked at her, I secretly thought, "It's just that I don't know whether or not I'll be able to pay you back."

Since I wanted her, didn't that mean that all my debts owing to her would be cleared?

As she had been so generous seeing me this first time after so many years, had she been thinking about me all along?

Unexpectedly, my heart leaped and I blushed. I don't know if she noticed. Of course, I didn't blush simply because I had discovered that she was much prettier than she had been several years ago. In that instant, I felt like a general, defeated in battle, who has returned to face his commander-in-chief.

Since that year when I had returned from my wanderings, I thought my heart was no longer capable of beating. I was certainly no damned ship's captain coming back in glory to his native home, with loads of money and treasures and smiling proudly, surrounded by the love and esteem of the crowds. In my pocket there were only a few clinking coins, and my heart which I had plucked out and put into my pocket to avoid misfortune and hurt; that heart which was once dignified, kind and honest, had accumulated scars, and then congealed and contracted to the size of a large walnut. Later I lost the ability to call upon my intuition in times of difficulty, because when I saw all the ravines lying everywhere in front of me, I thought that there was no way I could get across them....

"I want to marry you."

She looked stupefied, and suddenly began to cry. I knew that I had wronged her for ten thousand years.

"You probably say that kind of thing to every girl, as long as she can pay off your debts."

I trailed along behind her to the end of the corridor and into her seven-square-metre room which looked as though it had once been a toilet, and where she lived alone. I discovered that the border of fine down edging her hair, which was swept up high, was still the same as when we were children, even though she had gone through so many years of trials and hardship....

On the occasions when we met, she always kept a cautious attitude of not trusting others and not hoping for the trust of others. I wanted to use the fact of our years together as children, the fact of the glass marble with the red heart, as a means to get her to have a steady relationship with me, but she wouldn't have any of it. She was adamant that I should explain fully why I had to leave her that year to go wandering and why I hadn't come back for a hundred years; why, when I had come back, I hadn't had anything to do with her for another hundred years; and why, after those hundred years, upon our first meeting, I had asked her to help pay back money I owed.

I knew that there was a question which, if I could answer her, then I could answer the whole world. During my career as a beggar, I answered this question in a thousand different ways for more than a thousand different people. The people at that time wouldn't give anybody anything, so to make them give me something, I had to give them something first. I had to satisfy their grotesque curiosity.

Only on one occasion did I give a genuine and sincere answer, and that was to an old witch. She bought all the grain coupons, I had accumulated from ten days' begging for 30 *yuan*, which I felt at the time to be the fairest business transaction that had ever been or ever would be carried out, from the beginnings of the barter system to the end of the money economy.

For the first time, I explained how my old man had leapt like a diver to his death from the top of a six-storey building; how my old woman had tried to remove from his neck the wooden placard which was as big as a blackboard, and which had written on it a long list of accusations; I told the old witch how I ground my teeth when I watched my old woman doing this, and how the hate grew inside me, swelled up and almost burst my little nine-year-old heart; how I saw the blood from my old man's nose and mouth gush out in a foamy flood and pour onto the ground where it formed a large bloody patch; how I saw a drop of blood in my old man's ear, congealed and still; how I didn't cry.

The old witch and I sat together next to a stove heater in the waiting room of Xianyang train station. Outside, the cold winds whistled off the northwest highlands. As she listened to me recounting my story, with her two genuine witch's hands, she broke off the tips of some Xi'an brand cigarettes that she had collected, and put them on an old cloth she used for telling fortunes, on which were written things like the heavenly stems and earthly branches. She didn't ask me anything but merely listened indifferently. It was clear from her expression that she didn't think anything I was saying was particularly strange. I don't know why I was willing to confide in her. Perhaps it was simply because she didn't ask me anything. I also told her how later my old woman couldn't be found; how I received a letter from her, written with toothpaste on old paper, which she had got someone to bring from Gansu province. In the letter she urged me not to come and look for her under any circumstances. She told me to go and borrow some money from an aunt, but that aunt didn't know whether or not my old woman would come back alive, so she wouldn't even let me come in the door. As I waited outside, she gave me two left-over steamed buns and enough money to buy a tram ticket so I could make my way home again.

I told the old witch how the teachers at school always said I was no good, and how, whenever the Public Security Bureau felt like it, a couple of them would cart me off and ask me in what ways I had been influenced by my old man.

The old witch just listened without saying anything. Then she told me she had an eighteen-year-old son who still wet the bed. She wanted me to get a folk medicine prescription for her. She gave me an address on some damn big mountain in northern Shaanxi, and asked me to post the medicine once I'd tracked it down. She also asked me to take a letter to Beijing, a letter to a leading cadre in the Party Central Committee. One day, just before using the letter to wipe my backside, I squatted down in the latrine and, with some effort, read it through. In the letter she had written how the work unit that had come to work with her production team had forced the "poor and lower-middle peasants" to sell off their pots and pans and furniture and used the money to buy grain at a high price. The peasants presented it to the state as "surplus grain" and "contributed grain", and the higher authorities then sold the whole lot back to the "poor and lower-middle peasants" as "grain resold by the state to the place of production" and "emergency grain". She also wrote how she had been forced to stuff a load of rubbish into a grain crock, cover it with a thin layer of millet, and then on top of that place seven or eight eggs which a neighbour's lad had just rushed to her. These eggs had already secretly done the rounds of a hundred peasant homes. They had been passed around the old people's hands so much that they almost didn't hatch. And all because a Dazhai county inspection team had arrived on orders from above. In the letter she also wrote how the work unit had strung her up on the roof beams of her room and insisted that she was trying to sabotage the "In agriculture, learn from Dazhai" policy. As a result, she had been maimed, even though she had in the past been a member of the Red Army propaganda team, and had sung songs for Chairman Mao, and so on. Finally, she asked in her letter whether the leading cadre of the Party Central Committee still remembered her. She also said she now had no means of supporting herself. She could only do work considered "superstitious", so she wanted the leading cadre to send her 500 *yuan*.

Though I searched, I couldn't find any mention in the letter that she had slept with the "leading cadre" when she was young. As I read, I laughed, and when I finished laughing, I threw the letter into the latrine.

Later, I saw the old witch again in a hostel for drop-outs. This time she didn't want my grain coupons for love nor money and she also questioned me about the folk medicine. Luckily, I had on me a pencil that I used to sketch portraits in all sorts of places, so I used it to write out a prescription, which I then gave to her. On it was written: eight cobras and five tortoise eggs to be taken in one go. She looked at it, then rolled it up into a tube and stuffed it into the brim of her hat.

Later, in Jinzhou, I met someone who was also from Beijing like myself. He was an artist, shabbily dressed, with a worried expression. He was carrying a sack of flour and a quarter of a pig. Behind him was a young girl wearing glasses. She moved around impatiently, as though damn well wanting to find in this world of endless destruction some clean place, where they could calmly sit down to mix flour, cut up the meat and make dumplings.

That year, everything strange that could possibly happen, did happen.

I tried to think up a plan to trick him out of the sack of flour and quarter of a pig, which he was carrying on his badly hunched back, so that I could exchange them for a ticket to Gourd Island. Later, I discovered that the young girl's belly was not quite right. It turned out the artist had heard that in the northeast there was some "commanding officer" or other who had caused so much trouble that for several years the ordinary people hadn't laid eyes on white flour and pork, so the artist hoped that with his sack of flour and quarter of a pig he could go to this out of the way place and let the girl have an abortion.

Later the artist became a good friend. He rushed back to Beijing to get the girl settled; then he took a battered old painting case with some missing corners, and came looking for me, which made the girl hate me so much she said that if she saw me again, she would skin me alive.

As soon as I saw his paintings, I went crazy. I immediately threw the crayons and pencils I had used to paint the ordinary folk I encountered, into the sea off Gourd Island, because his paintings expressed what I wanted to express but could never express in a lifetime; a multitude of colours that still constantly damn well seethe and surge in my heart. Once, feeling in the right mood, I told him all over again everything that I had told the old witch. Like her, he listened without saying a word, his two eyes dull and lifeless.

Unfortunately, he became, in reality, a burden to me. He had no experience at begging, but at the same time he was extremely fond of drink. All I could do was tell him how to beg from bloody courting couples. But he was never any good at differentiating such people from anyone else. On one occasion, a young married couple who looked like they were courting, but in fact had come outside to kiss and cuddle because they didn't have their own home to do it in, beat him up on the Qingdao sea-wall.

When I heard what was going on, I rushed up, and, from behind, kicked the stinking guy into the sea.

Several years later, the artist became a big-shot mathematician. He often came to see me, and told me how, that year, when he saw my crazy expression of joy and bitterness, he too became crazy. I told him of my original intentions, and he replied that if I had tricked him out of the sack of flour and quarter of pig, he would have had to hang the girl with the glasses with his own trouser belt.

I knew that there was a question which, if I could give the answer to her, I would tell the whole world, even though the world, hadn't in fact, asked me the question.

I wanted to tell her what kind of person I was; that I was weak and useless, that I was completely incapable of transcending the emotional barriers I'd created over the years; that I was completely incapable of any responsibility; but I also wanted to tell her how I still kept the pure and sincere love I had for her when we were children. I didn't want to wreck her peaceful life like a bull in a china shop. I also wanted to tell her that I was now an adult; I was going to abandon the grievances I'd been accumulating; I was not going to continue brooding over the break-up of my family and the deaths and disappearances of family members, over the vicissitudes of my life during my years of wandering, over my imprisonment at a tender age. No, it's not because all these things are in the past, too far in the past. The crux of the matter is that there is no way I can bring everything to an end. I was too frightened and cowardly. I would go on living.

But there was something that I thought I could explain clearly to her. Many years ago, on the day before I left home, I went to look for her. She was with a group of little girls, playing with a rubber band skipping rope and in high spirits. She seemed too busy to pay any attention to me, so I went to look for her mom. I discovered that her young mother had become ugly; her hair was cut really short, and she was in the process of using a hacksaw blade to saw off the high heels of her beautiful shoes, one pair after another. When she realized I had come in, she ruffled my hair and burst out crying.... As I recall now, it was just like a film, say, the clumsiest scene from a clumsy film, such as *Cowshed* or *Persecution*. But although there were a lot of similarities, I just couldn't believe that any of the people making the film had ever really been "persecuted". If I had made that kind of film, I would only film one scene, repeatedly film one scene, that of a young mother, whose hair had been shorn, sawing off the heels of her shoes with half a hacksaw blade, sawing until her face was covered in sweat. I wouldn't even film how, in the past, she liked to buy all kinds of shoes, how she loved to wear all kinds of beautiful leather shoes when she went out dancing....

I told her mom that I was going to look for my "uncle".

There was a damn neighbour's kid who always used to show off about his uncle, and use this uncle to try and make me feel small. He said that his uncle had climbed over snowy mountains and crossed grasslands. He also said that the company commander in the film *Red Sun*, who always carried a knife and rode a horse, was his uncle. I always wanted to invent an "uncle" who was a private adviser to the Boxers to get the better of him, but before I had the chance, he and his father left for Anhui.

I really did go to look for my "uncle". I went around the whole damn country and discovered that there were "uncles" all over the place. Needless to say, there were those who had been important advisers to the Boxers, those who had been Liu Bang[2]....

I said that I had gradually grown up and become an adult, and I was going to abandon all those accumulated grievances and conscientiously consider how I was to carry on living. I wanted her to be my wife, but it really wasn't easy to get this across to her fully. She spent much of her time telling her fortune with playing cards, and she also took me along to a young sorcerer's house so that he could read my palms. I never thought that this young sorcerer would turn out to have such extraordinary skill. He concentrated his gaze on the back of my head for a long time; he concentrated so hard that my scalp tightened. He also took my left hand and scrutinized it carefully, as though he were looking for something. If at that time there had been an ant crawling over my hand, from the expression in the sorcerer's eyes, he would certainly have followed it with his gaze all the way to the Shandong peninsula.

"There aren't many people who have the same kind of fate as you. Your fate is that of someone who will roam all over the world!" He practically said I had a rebel's bone at the back of my head, damn it!

Upon hearing the sorcerer's words, she became cold towards me. I was momentarily dumbfounded, and could only listen to him going on about the Yin and the Yang.

"Any illness destroys the balance of Yin and Yang. Because I understand balance, I am never ill."

---

[2] Founding emperor of the Han dynasty (202 BC–AD 220).

I found that in the less than half an hour that we had been sitting in his home, he had been to the toilet ten times. I asked whether he had diarrhoea. He remarked modestly "Yesterday I ate too much crab. Crab is Yin, so it has cold properties."

Because the young sorcerer had said that I was a wanderer, she prevaricated for more than ten thousand years and wouldn't agree to marry me. In order to clarify things, I decided to go and see him alone. I heard he was from an old well-known family in the traditional Chinese medicine line. He was not only studying traditional Chinese medicine by himself, but also, in order to become a doctor specializing in Western medicine in the future, he was expending great efforts to study Latin and such things. This time I decided to go and ask him to feel my pulse, to see whether or not I and my beloved girlfriend were closely linked as far as our pulses went.

I went to look for him early one morning and saw him amongst some trees in front of his house. He was striding in all directions, and in his hands he was holding a book which he was reading out at great length, looking decidedly pleased with himself. From his manner, you would think that what he had in his hand was not some Latin text book, but *The Analects* written on bamboo.

He showed me into his room and, as he talked to me, dipped a large painting brush into a dish of clear water and wrote some characters on a sheet of white paper. This startled me; I thought he was going to do some kind of sorcery. Then he explained that the calligrapher, Wang Xizhi,[3] used to do the same thing. Later, he really showed off his skills to me; on the day that we were married, he made us a present of eight characters he had written: "Where the water is clean, wash your braids, where the water is dirty, wash your feet." Because I couldn't understand what the characters meant, I didn't bother about whether or not they were appropriate, I just hung them up.

It took me all of a hundred years or more to recognize those eight characters. Luckily, in the days after we'd got married I was preoccupied with other things, but that's all for later.

---

[3] c. 307–365. China's most renowned calligrapher.

"Damn it, next time you read my palm in front of her, can't you say something nice about me?" I stated quite clearly without beating around the bush. When I said this, my eyes must have glinted menacingly, because as soon as I'd finished, he ran inside and came back again after a while. I could vaguely make out a vegetable knife tucked behind his back. I was frightened, frightened that he was the kind of person who would know the simple principle that he who strikes the first blow is the strongest. Because in my pocket I only had a two centimetre fruit knife.

This time he really did have a change of heart. He said how single-minded I was about love, so single-minded that I was like that disabled foreign poetess. He also said that I would father eight children. Whoever married me would certainly give birth to octuplets....

Having gone through countless twists and turns, and the hazards of the fortune-telling and pulse-taking at the young sorcerer's home, my greatest desire finally came to fruition. We set up a small home in her little seven-square-metre room.

But in order to get used to the new situation, she and I were going to have to enlist the services of a dancing teacher, because, whenever we walked into the room, whatever movement we wanted to make, we always had to take dancing steps. Except disco, we danced every dance you care to mention. Before we were practised enough to become immortals of dance, our thighs and calves were black and blue from banging the bedhead, the table legs or the corners of the chairs.

In spite of all that, in the beginning, we lived quite happily. Since a kind of relaxed harmony permeated each day from start to finish, we "closed our door to the outside world", and felt that there was nothing in the world for us to envy or be jealous about, even if there was some adolescent out there who had eight rooms to live in.

From the time her mother died and her father "remarried", she had been under the guardianship of a group of old women from the neighbourhood where my parents' living quarters belonging to their work unit had been situated. From the age of ten, she took part in political studies organized by the neighbourhood committee, right up to the age of fifteen, when she entered a neighbourhood factory to complete the final part of her childhood education.

I don't know whether or not her attitude of keeping a low profile and inactivity in response to everything in life was connected with this kind of education. During those years, did she use that guileless sense of humour as the best weapon to ward off despair and a feeling of isolation, until finally it became a habit?

In the early days, she would often rejoice that we had a little seven-square-metre room. But I found that if I had to continue living in this small room for any length of time, there would come a day when I would definitely bash my brains against the wall, just like that minister of Yue[4] who, clasping the He family jade, knocked his head against a pillar in the Qin palace.

But getting the bearing factory she worked in to provide us with a room was more difficult than achieving a damn reconciliation between the bourgeoisie and the proletariat. I'd heard that only five bearing factories were needed to supply the entire country, but in fact there were probably more than 5,000. Every day I looked forward to the factory closing down, so that my wife could do something more worthwhile.

She fascinated me and moved me emotionally in many different ways. I would often observe some of her movements to piece together and repair the fragmented impressions she had left in my heart as a child.

For example, she would excitedly look through an old book by Victor Hugo, and when she found a particularly good passage, she would pull me over to read those few lines too, and then I would think back to when we were children, and how I stole from home an album full of pictures of all kinds of forests for us both to look at. Those forests were painted in such a way that you really wanted to

---

[4] The author has distorted the historical facts somewhat. The jade he refers to belonged to the He family, who lived in the state of Zhao during the Warring States period (453–221 BC). The king of Qin demanded the jade, whreupon a senior minister from Zhao brought it to the palace. The minister, however, then vigorously defended Zhao's right to keep the jade, and the king was so impressd by his impassioned plea that he allowed the minister to take it back to Zhao.

run into them, bringing with you a young girl wearing little red shoes and a little white dress to play hide-and-seek.

And, when later her temper worsened and she would become enraged in our little seven-square-metre room, like the Empress Dowager Cixi, cursing that one of the shoes I had taken off had been flung to Mexico and the other thrown to Morocco, I would think back to how, when we were young, I was sorely grieved when she caught sight of my feet, which were as dirty as a black bear's backside.

Later, my wife became more and more strange.

Though we had tried everything, she finally realized that we would never become immortals of dance. Then things really began going wrong, just because at this point, I was at last gradually starting to feel at ease.

In the beginning, she cleaned the room every day, and fixed it up as though she were expecting a visit from a sanitation inspection team at any moment. Later she began dropping comments about my habits that froze with irony and burnt with satire. She said that I "acted" like an artist, but that, in fact, I was nothing but a big shit. She said such things so often that I wondered whether or not she was having an early menopause due to all her misfortunes as a child. Because during this time, whenever I saw her, her most beautiful expression was when there no expression.

Whenever I indulged in loud and empty talk with friends in our little room, and went about bare-foot and bare-chested, she would look at me with a cold, mocking expression, then she would take an old chair downstairs and place it under the large tree, where she would sit staring. When everyone else had gone, and only the two of us were left, she would look at me, and I would look at her, and we would both feel uncomfortable. To break the stalemate she would take my dirty socks and shirts full of cigarette burn holes and throw them at me, all the while cursing, "I was fine here by myself, so why did you have to come barging over? So, this is the happy life you promised me?!" At such times, I would be like a damn idiot, laughing stupidly, my eyes blank and lifeless, my I.Q. probably zero.

One year the winter was so cold that it could freeze a stove heater solid. I was at home, engrossed in scrubbing a pan. I was scrubbing so hard that my face was covered in sweat. This was all because ten days previously I had been slow-cooking a pan of rice, and the bottom of it had got burned as black as a dogskin plaster, spoiling my wife's appetite. Because of this, she hadn't eaten rice for ten days and was waiting for me to clean the pan.

Then a genteel young woman appeared on the scene. She had heard that I was really great, a master, an extraordinary sage, so she had come especially to ask me about life. My wife immediately went out of the room and paced back and forth in the long corridor waiting for us to hurry up and finish.

The woman first mentioned a whole list of people and asked whether or not I knew them. Among them were a few I knew from last century, when they lost all their marbles to me. Then, my mom became suspicious; she pulled open my drawer and the marbles rolled about on the bottom. She said there were too many germs on them, and insisted that I throw them all away. So I buried them in the same way that I would later plant corn in northern Shandong, but I kept one, one with a red heart, which I gave to her when we were still children.

These people had now all become various kinds of "masters". Some of them had shaved off their hair in order to shock, and had been invited by university students to give speeches.

"I don't know them, I don't know them," I told her modestly, because I was worried that if I said I knew them, swear words would come rushing out of my mouth, and I was afraid that the young woman would think I was crude.

Finally, she asked me if I knew how to extract and refine magic potions from the Immortal Ball plant. I stared at her, speechless, then quickly asked her to tell me more. She was also extremely modest in her reply, saying, "At the moment, my efforts are only at the experimental stage."

From that time on, she would probably never again think that I was some damn great sage.

She left, and I quickly told my wife to come in, fearing she would die of cold. My wife had heard every word we said. She was completely fed up with everything, and on top of that, the dirty pan that I still hadn't cleaned made her feel even more vexed. She didn't say a thing as she took her dancing steps, moving and weaving, pushing objects out of her way, all in an unusually nimble fashion. She got to the bookcase and took a book from it, leafed through several pages, and, now in familiar territory, began to read aloud softly.

"Dear brothers! The test of fire has come down upon your heads, but don't think this is strange. On the contrary, you should rejoice, because Jesus suffers with you.... Amen!"

I looked closely and discovered that she was holding a copy of the Bible. I asked her why she had started praying. She said it was to suppress her feelings of anger, so as to avoid killing me in a fit of temper.

I finally discovered what was behind all this, why we could never get along well. It was because we always had to take dancing steps, as though we were wearing damn red dancing shoes. It was because of the little seven-square-metre room. Our dancing steps had utterly exhausted us, and the limited space of seven square metres made breathing difficult.

By the way, I have to say, I'm not one for contesting and competing with others, yet my wife always took great pains to use a phrase from the Bible to help me see what was the right thing to do—"God helps those who help themselves". I had to help myself. So, one day I barged into the office of my superiors at work. I told them I had taken a wife, that I wanted to set up a home, that I wanted to put in that home a big wide bed, that I wanted to hang above the bed a family planning propaganda poster, that I wanted a room.

They immediately burst out laughing. They had always looked upon me as a freak, almost everyone thought I was abnormal, they reckoned that I was a higher species two-legged animal wanting somewhere to keep out the wind and rain, a place in which to multiply, that I would probably think I had been given a room just so that I could demolish it, and then go peddling off on a three-wheeled cart to sell off stuff like broken bricks.

"Wait!" They said when they'd finished laughing.

I'm a very patient person, I really love waiting. I have already got used to that kind of waiting, the outcome of which often leaves you not knowing whether to laugh or cry. For example, you wait for a beautiful girl to marry, and as a consequence, you wait eighty years. Just when you reach a hundred, she arrives. Surprised, you ask yourself how she could have become an old woman. As another example, you wait for a room; in the process of waiting you're not aware that you are slowly becoming a gross freak. By the time you have become so big that each step you take treads down the earth more than twenty centimetres, your boss tells you in a matter-of-fact way that such-and-such a place has a room for you, it's eight square metres, things like that; and you travel day and night at double speed to get to the place, only to find that your wife can't even get her red-painted toe into it. If you so much as gave a gentle fart, the room would come tumbling down.

In another sense, waiting brings me a feeling of consolation and conceals the dread I have about life, conceals my uselessness. Every time I feel useless and weak, I mockingly say to myself, "Wait!"

In the end, the two of us virtually became great immortals of dance. There is after all "nothing in this world that is so difficult it can't be achieved!" The only thing to be fearful of is patient people! If you were to see how the two of us opened the door to our room and walked towards the bed, and towards our eating place; how I walked towards my bottle of liquor and she walked towards a half-finished sweater; if you saw us twisting and turning you would certainly have applauded our exquisite dancing.

Later we opened up our door and got to know a little more about the world outside. She began to remark on what size room so-and-so had, what so-and-so was like. She also started making tentative future plans for us, when we did move house; where it would be most appropriate to put the bed; what would be the most tasteful place for the "Eight Immortals" dining table; what would be the most elegant place to put the bookcase, full of its Bibles and Analects; which would be the ideal place for that large Ming vase so that it could best express the rich and great spirit of China's traditional culture. Almost every day she concocted a new variation so that I couldn't keep up. Once she realized that, of her more than a hundred plans, there wasn't one that I could recall, she became enraged and kicked me out the door. I could only wheel out my faithful and trusty bike and go and find a little bar.

Everyone who has seen this bicycle of mine says it looks like me; some simply say that it is me. But that's not purely because it's on the verge of rusting into two iron circles. The main reason is that every conceivable place on the bike sticks out or has developed edges.

I leapt onto my bike and rushed out into the street, noisily ringing my bell that had been knocked oval. At almost every intersection I hit a damn red light. Whenever there was a car in front of me, whether it was travelling quickly or slowly, I always overtook it like a madman; it's a habit of mine.

Eventually I realized that there would always be cars ahead of me, cars that I'd never be able to overtake....

I knew that there would come a day when, because I overtook cars in this crazy way, I would crash into a bus full of passengers, my blood and flesh would become a mangled mess, and I'd die.

Perhaps I would get knocked over and die, but the doctors would still carry me into an ambulance, siren blaring. The driver and the doctors would all be absolutely clear about this damn simple truth, that is, there's a dead person on board, a young fellow who gambled with his life. But they would still drive the ambulance, siren blaring, so that they could show my corpse to the traffic police and have a good laugh, so that they could go through all the red lights along the way without having to stop, so that they could finish work early and go home for dinner, so that they could tell their wives and children, the old and the young, as they ate, "Another one was knocked down and killed today."

All that time, I'd be lying on a dirty stretcher in some freezing cold hospital mortuary, and I'd be thinking, "When I was still damn alive I never could cross a red light. It's only now that I'm dead that I can damn well for once break the rules without having to pay a fine....

Everything of mine is like me. I have a digital watch with a liquid crystal display, which is more or less as mad as myself. Every ten to fifteen days this watch displays 88.88. I have racked my brains, but can't think what time this 88.88 actually is. So instead I have to use the left side of my nose to tell me when it's day, and the right side when it's night.

I love this watch so much, it drives me crazy. Because of it, I always go especially to buy a whole box of pins, then, with a feeling of reverence and awe, I prod it every day, but however much I prod, the 88.88 fails to appear. Then, when the last pin in the box has become blunt with all the prodding, and I am about to smash the watch to pieces and throw it in the river to feed the fish, this mysterious time re-appears, whereupon I go off to buy another box of pins....

We spent each day waiting. Waiting had become the only thing in my wife's life. She waited anxiously, as Empress Dowager Cixi had waited, after fleeing to Chengde, for Waldersee[5] to decide to disperse his troops. Even before going to the toilet, my wife would say, "After we've moved we won't ever need to use this stinking toilet again."

That toilet really was unspeakably wonderful, even more stinking than the latrine I had been squatting in when I had used the old witch's letter to wipe my backside. If you had the chance to be a guest in our home, and you wanted to use the toilet, you wouldn't need to ask me where the toilet was. You could just take a deep breath, and follow the smell around a few corners and you'd find it.

I knew that if we continued in this way, my wife would go mad. So, while waiting, I also began to be enterprising. I considered all humanly conceivable methods, stopping just short of things that the law dreamed up by humans didn't permit. But the hope of moving still remained vague, like a four-year-old dreaming of taking a wife. So, in order to dampen her enthusiasm, I did my utmost to get her to recall the happy scenes of the past. When we lay on our bed thinking of bygone times, I would tell her about all the interesting things that had happened during my "glorious Long March" and my wanderings in the world.

---

[5] Field Marshall Count von Waldersee, commander-in-chief of the allied foreign forces holding Peking, following the Boxer Uprising in 1900.

I began to tell her about that stretch of barren and desolate earth which had three trees instead of a place name. I told her of all my experiences at the time, wanting to use those rich and magnificent experiences to arouse her interest, so that she could temporarily forget all the vexations brought about by this seven square metres of space.

I told her about a certain October afternoon several years ago. I was sitting on a high, prominent yellow-earth slope by the Yellow River where it flows through the central area of China. Down below were mingled the silt of the highlands and the great yellow waves rolling from east to west, passing dead twigs and withered leaves along the way.

Looking beyond the uneven hills that were clustered into a stretch of ravines and ridges, I could see the edge of the Yellow River disappear into the distant, mysterious horizon. I described in detail the boundless land beneath the vast skies of the northwest. I recalled how over all those years I had used those feelers in my heart that were more numerous and more sensitive than a butterfly's to experience and understand life now, life in the future, as well as time and space. I became deeply cognizant of the fact that everything a person has, and everything he is capable of having, is, as far as a certain dominant force in Heaven is concerned, damn insignificant.

From that time on, I decided to abandon all the hate I had held in my belly. I knew that I would begin to adopt a light-hearted and detached attitude and tread a new path in life.

Behind me, ten or so kilometres away, was the only piece of land with alkaline soil, barely enough to allow anyone to eke out an existence. On this land lived a group of girls at the most lovely age who had come from a number of big cities all over China. You could tell from the plain weave of their yellow uniforms that they were not true soldiers. They had the pious demeanour of nuns. With solemn expressions on their faces they planted old corn which was harvested once a year. It was said that in one of the years, one *mu* of land only produced eighteen *jin* of corn after being planted with more than two hundred *jin*. Probably not so much was required for planting, but then an educated female youth, with the glorious title of "PLA political instructor" arrived, and she damn well forced everyone, in the season when the old corn was almost ripe, to replant, one by one, the seeds that hadn't sprouted and those that had sprouted but had died young....

I've already said that year everything strange that could possibly happen, did happen. If in Heaven there really is a God, he must have no time to do anything else but stare down at the world below, at that place called China. Because everything that happens there would cheer him up more than anything else. If God's is by nature optimistic and if he has a good sense of humour, then he must definitely be damn well pleased to death, Amen!

There was a small shop there, and in it was a beautiful Qingdao girl who was the "boss woman". Sometimes, I would go to this shop and buy a packet of Grassland cigarettes for eight cents.

The kindly girls there took me under their wing; my arrival had created waves. With the exception of the "political instructor", all of the girls were willing to take me as their "little brother". During the many days that they took care of me, the "boss woman" taught me how to ride....

On the day I left them, they lined up to see me off. The "boss woman" shed some tears.

So that some day they would remember that wandering youth who looked like a skeleton, so that some day they would remember those skeleton feet, covered in dirt, that looked as though they had walked all over the world, so that some day they would remember that skeleton life who spent some depressing days with them during those sad and bitter times, I used those few skeleton-like crayons of mine to draw a portrait of those skeleton-like girls....

Then I left, wearing my boat-like moccasins, the bottoms of my trousers flapping like streamers....

I promised my wife that if in the future I was really able to write a novel or something, I would write especially for her about the place with the three trees, and I would guarantee that after reading it, she wouldn't be able to stop talking about it.

Every evening I chatted endlessly to my wife about all the gossip and other such farting matters. As she listened, sometimes her eyes would fill with tears, sometimes she couldn't stop laughing. In the end my storytelling really did dampen the raging fire she felt in her heart from all the waiting.

Eventually, there was no need for me to tell stories, because finally we got a new room. As I say it, you might not believe me, but that room was ten square metres bigger than our old one. At this rate, we could even hold a damn dance party or something.

I bet that the impression you have of my and my wife's dancing is that we had had professional training.

It wasn't at all difficult to come by this room. My wife had an "uncle" who, as luck would have it, had the same surname as she. He allowed us to live in the room that he was going to give to his five-year-old daughter when she married many years hence, on the condition that he could take my wife as his "niece", and "bring her up". Fortunately, my wife had no dad or mom. On the day when he came to our door, I almost chased him away, because as soon as he got in, he started calling himself "uncle". I thought he'd come to play some joke. My wife tried her hardest, but after a long while, she still couldn't place him. Finally, he mentioned that when my wife was three years old he had given her a fruit lolly. My wife, realizing that his visit could be to our benefit, said that she faintly remembered him. It was only then that I put down the broom I was holding.

Within an hour we'd gone through all the formalities. Within five hours we'd moved house. My wife was surprised to find that all the plans she'd made designing the positioning of the furniture could become a reality. Now, all that was left for her to do was to use those plans to torture me. I really regretted that when I was buying all this furniture, I didn't fix something like bicycle wheels to it all.

Fortunately, we no longer needed to dance.

But the way my wife walked around the new room left me speechless; even though a long time had elapsed since we had moved, she was still walking in the old way. Only after taking two or three steps would she suddenly realize what was happening, and relax her movements. I also found to my surprise that her steps had become strange and unfamiliar!

On such occasions, we would look at each other, and laugh sardonically as if as an excuse to console ourselves.

To lessen her sadness, we later decided to move the furniture around. In order to get used to the place more quickly, we adopted a whole series of measures. In the process of moving the furniture we dropped the Ming porcelain vase on the floor and it smashed to pieces....

But none of the measures were effective. We went through the same rigmarole almost every day. Finally, I realized that there was no way we could live in a large room, because we lacked the right consciousness. All our measures were in form only. We lacked the right consciousness for living in a large room!

I think that if we had come directly from a rough and desolate place to live in this big room, perhaps things would have been better. But we had that long history of living in a seven-square-metre room. It's difficult to express in words the unhappiness that seven square metres can create. Perhaps there are some who would be willing to go back to such a small place to experience again that kind of pleasant warmth and cosiness. I had had enough, and so had my wife!

Though we continued to believe that there would eventually come a day when we would get settled in, this slow and lengthy process made her extremely unhappy. Added to this was the neighbour, a young lad; he was always in his room, either playing a music tape over and over, or counting out in a loud voice, "One, two, three, four". It was only then I realized that everything else about the room was all right, but it didn't really keep out the noise, which meant that it was easy for the outside world to intrude.

The piece of music was actually not bad, it was just that, near the end, for God knows what reason, the piano is suddenly replaced by a barrage of stringed instruments, which is really hard to take. Finally, one day, my wife asked me what damn piece of music it was. *An American in Paris*. I had previously received some instruction in such matters. "What the hell is this American doing in Paris?" "After tiring himself out having fun, he is sleeping with his arms around a young Parisian girl. The composer wants to wake him up."
"Why doesn't he use an alarm clock?"

I certainly didn't know. She should go and ask Gershwin.

The neighbour was very ugly.

Each unit had two rooms for two lots of people. We shared with our neighbour a kitchen, a toilet and an entrance hall. In the hall, I put a pile of junk in the space that I thought belonged to us, and left empty shelf space for him that was three times what we had. But he didn't put anything there, and would under no circumstances stop for even a second in the hall. He always hurriedly pulled out his key, and after opening the door a crack so that he could squeeze himself in, he would immediately close it again. It was really strange; on the odd occasion when we did bump into each other, it was always when we were coming in the door together. Since I and my wife had come to live in the unit, there had never even been an occasion when we and he had wanted to use the toilet at the same time. In the mornings, when I was in the kitchen washing myself and rinsing my mouth, there was no point in hoping he would come in. If I deliberately dawdled, he might really force himself not to come in for a whole day, even though he would be in his room holding all the things he needed for washing and for brushing his teeth, anxious, like a damn grasshopper running around crazily in circles.

It was only after I had been living there for seven or eight days that I first saw him. If it wasn't for the fact that on his window overlooking the street there was a dark reddish-purple velveteen curtain that was always closed, whether it was day or night, I wouldn't know that I damn well had a neighbour.

His two eyes bulged, like a big frog. His upper lids were completely covered in broken veins; the flesh of his two cheeks hung down slackly, forming sunken semi-circles at the corner of his mouth. The sides of his nose were so broad they looked as if they would submerge the bridge of his nose at any moment. His front teeth protruded, propping up his upper lip a full one centimetre, and this, with his nose, formed a risible triangle.

On one occasion, he grinned at me, no doubt as a kind of greeting, then quickly regained his original manner, as though he was afraid that if he continued to grin I would steal away his lovable expression. I put on a radiant smile, but I felt uneasy, and didn't dare look at him, mostly out of respect. I guessed he must have been extremely sensitive about his own face.

Every evening, quite inexplicably, he would count away, modulating his tone every so often, until eventually, it became very distressing for me. Finally, one day, I rushed into that coffin-like room of his, wanting to know what it was he was counting. But all I saw was him curled up in a large reclining chair, his two eyes staring straight ahead at a clock hanging on the wall opposite. He was counting each swing of its pendulum. There was a pile of foreign-language books on a table.

He politely asked me to sit down. I was a bit frightened, because I thought that he might be mentally disturbed.

"I'm doing research on the second law of thermodynamics," he said, fixing me with a stare. His two eyes were so bright, they were frightening. I then had my first experience of a conversation with someone who was mentally deranged. "Entropy. Do you understand, entropy?" "I don't," I told him frankly. "That is to say, all energy flows from a higher to a lower density. There will come a day when it will finish flowing, then there will be no energy left, and everything will be in a state of equilibrium. The world and human society will all be destroyed. Look." He pointed to the clock on the wall. "It's not going for no reason. It's going because you give it a clock spring, you give it energy, and only then can it go. When the energy has been used up it will stop. If you keep constantly providing it with energy, but you don't keep providing yourself with energy, for example, if you don't eat or drink etc., you'll die. That is to say, your energy will stop flowing from a higher to a lower density. There will no longer be any high or low, but a plane, and you will have died!"

"But the energy in the world is limitless. So the situation you're talking about will never arise."

My interest had really been aroused, and I felt so happy I wanted to dance for joy.

Sometimes you can find something about which you can really talk nonsense, and people will actually listen to you. You don't need to think about grammar or logic, and you don't need to think about whether or not other people understand your nonsense. Going on interest alone, you blindly rabbit on, pouring out a whole bellyful of bad luck and rationality in order to damn well mock it.

He became anxious. I could see that he wasn't good at debate, but in my belly was a really mischievous fellow.

"One of these days the whole universe will become totally pitch-black," he shouted.

On the basis of his rationale, I let my imagination range without limit: one day the energy of the sun would be exhausted, all of the water in the great Yangtze River would have finished flowing from higher to lower; neither would there be anything like electricity, because the wind had stopped blowing, the coal had all been dug up, the water had stopped flowing, so what would we use to generate electricity? Perhaps everything would really become pitch-black like he said. Perhaps that strange time of 88.88 which appears on that strange watch of mine would really come about? Perhaps there just wouldn't be any time at all?

"What are you studying?" he asked me impatiently. From his manner, it seemed as though, if I answered incorrectly, he would surely jump out of the building in his sadness and disappointment.

The verb "to study" really has become fashionable out of all proportion. People study away like bees in a hive. They don't first plan things for themselves. They just study and study. They spend their best years studying and then, when they've studied for a lifetime, they discover that they haven't actually learned anything. What am I studying?

I told him that in the past I had thought of studying equations, but later I discovered that before me there had been Russell; then I thought of studying things like making soft drinks by a process of acid-alkali neutralization, but then I discovered that before me there had been Faraday; then I wanted to study the guitar, but I knew that before me there had been Beethoven; I also studied writing novels, but then I heard that in front of me were traditional masters and behind Futurist masters, in countless numbers, and all eyeing their prey covetously; so I studied "having a nervous break down", but then I discovered that before me there were a whole lot of Western AIDS sufferers; and what's more, they no longer damn well wore American jeans....

So, when at this point I tried quickly to bring things to a halt, I found my blood had dried up, my eyes had gone blind, and my back was bent.

What am I studying?

I don't know whether or not I too am mad.

So, I said that I was thinking of studying teasing cotton....

He was really disappointed to hear this. He said that I should be studying like him.

I gave him some sincere encouragement. I told him that if he wanted to achieve something, he should go about it as though he were in a fight. The key to the whole thing was that you should grab hold of the opposition and not let go of him, even if he is a big man seven *chi* tall, even if he knocks you to the ground. As long as he doesn't kill you, you can crawl back onto your feet and continue to grab hold of him and not let him go. Right up until you have the opportunity to inflict a fatal blow, the key is to hold him tight and not let go.

When I was about to leave, I told him there was no need for him to go on endlessly counting the strokes of the pendulum, because it swings sixty times every minute. So if he really wanted to know, he could calculate it for himself. It hadn't occurred to me that on hearing this he would start to cry, and, just like a woman, say I was cruel, since I had told him the solution to his riddle and he would no longer need to guess it himself.

I went across to comfort him, but he grabbed something from the table and threw it at me, at the same time cursing, "F… you!"

I picked up what he'd thrown and looked at it. It was a tape of the original version of *An American in Paris*.

When I returned home I told my wife what had happened. She complained about all the rubbish I'd said to him about fighting being comparable to achieving something. She reckoned that kind of talk would only add to his mental illness.

One evening, I was lying on the bed, reading a book and smoking. I asked my wife to empty the ashtray which was full of cigarette butts. Coming back, she began, as was her habit, to take the dancing steps that she had used before we moved to the new place. I looked at her in surprise. She took two steps then suddenly realized.

A look of panic came over her, then she threw herself wailing, onto the bed.

I comforted her and then she suddenly sat up. Her eyes were full of tears and she looked at me with a pitiful expression.

"I can't stand it, I can't stand it. Let's just move back to our old place as soon as possible."

I gazed at her confused and helpless demeanour, and was suddenly seized by an impulse. I felt that she had never looked so moving. I threw myself on her, wanting to be affectionate. She kicked me angrily, and swore at me, saying that I was a bastard who always did the wrong thing at the wrong time....

I have always wanted to learn how to do the right thing at the right time, and study it with all those people who already know, but I never seem to manage it. Perhaps what that young sorcerer who was studying calligraphy and Latin said about me was right, and I really am destined to roam all over the world.

WILD PEONY PTY LTD BOOK PUBLISHERS A.C.N. 002 714 276
PO BOX 636 BROADWAY NSW 2007 AUSTRALIA
Fax: 61 2 9566 1052

International Distribution: University of Hawaii Press, 2840 Kolowalu Street, Honolulu Hawaii 96822. Fax: 1 808 988-6052

• *Shijin: Autobiography of the Poet Kaneko Mitsuharu, 1895-1975*. Introduction and translations by A. R. Davis; edited by A. D. Syrokomla-Stefanowska. University of Sydney East Asian Series, No. 1; ISBN: 0 9590735 3 1; 1988; 324 pp.; hardcover: AUS $40.00. (AVAILABLE WILD PEONY ONLY.)

• Tanizaki Jun'ichiro, *A Cat, Shozo and Two Women*. Translated by Matsui Sakuko. University of Sydney East Asian Series, No. 2; ISBN: 0 9590735 5 8; 150 pp.; 1988; hardcover: AUS $27.95; softcover: AUS $12.95. (AVAILABLE WILD PEONY ONLY.)

• Yang Lian, *Masks and Crocodile: A Contemporary Chinese Poet and His Poetry*. Introduction and translations by Mabel Lee; 12 coloured illustrations by Li Liang. University of Sydney East Asian Series, No. 3; ISBN: 0 9590735 7 4; 1990; 146 pp.; softcover: AUS $25.00. (AVAILABLE WILD PEONY ONLY.)

• *Gen'ei: Selected Poems of Nishiwaki Junzaburo, 1894-1982*. Translations by Yasuko Claremont. University of Sydney East Asian Series, No. 4; ISBN: 0 9590735 8 2; 1991; 120 pp.; softcover: AUS $19.95

• *Seven Stories of Modern Japan*. Edited by Leith Morton. Translations by H. Clarke, S. Matsui and L. Morton. University of Sydney East Asian Series, No. 5; ISBN: 0 9590735 9 0; 1991; 88 pp.; softcover: AUS $19.95

• *Kyunyŏ-jŏn: The Life, Times and Songs of a Tenth Century Korean Buddhist Monk*. Translated and annotated by Adrian Buzo and Tony Prince. University of Sydney East Asian Series, No. 6; ISBN: 0 646 14772 2; 1993; 142 pp.; softcover: AUS $25.00

• *Modernity in Asian Art*. Edited by John Clark. University of Sydney East Asian Series, No. 7; ISBN: 0 646 14773 0; 1993; 350 pp.; softcover: AUS $37.50

• *The Chinese Femme Fatale: Short Stories of the Ming Period*. Translations by Anne McLaren. University of Sydney East Asian Series, No. 8; ISBN: 0 646 14924 5; 1994; 102 pp.; softcover: AUS $22.95

• *Visiting the Mino Kilns*. Translation and introduction by Janet Barriskill. University of Sydney East Asian Series, No. 9; ISBN: 0 646 2042 4 6; 1995; 90 pp. + colour plates 56 pp.; hardcover: AUS $65.00

Mark Elvin, *Another History: Essays on China from a European Perspective*. University of Sydney East Asian Series No. 10; ISBN: 0 646 2041 3 0; 1996; pp.; softcover. AUS $47.50

• Mabel Lee and Meng Hua, *Cultural Dialogue and Misreading*. University of Sydney World Literature Series No. 1; ISBN: 0 9586526 1 9; 1996; 500 pp.; softcover: AUS $45.00

• Mabel Lee and A. D. Syrokomla-Stefanowska (eds), *Modernization of the Chinese Past*; University of Sydney School of Asian Studies Series, No. 1; ISBN: 0 867 5865 8 3; 1993; 208 pp.; softcover: AUS $25.00

• Kam Louie, *Between Fact and Fiction: Essays on Post-Mao Literature and Society*; ISBN: 0 9590735 6 6; 1989; 149 pp.; softcover: AUS $22.75. (AVAILABLE WILD PEONY ONLY.)

• Lily Xiao Hong Lee, *The Virtue of Yin: Studies on Chinese Women*; ISBN 0 646 1492 5 3; 1994; 117 pp.; softcover: AUS $18.95

• A. D. Syrokomla-Stefanowska, *A Classical Chinese Reader*, ISBN: 0 9586526 0 0; 192 pp.; softcover: AUS $40.00

• Mabel Lee and Zhang Wu-ai, *Putonghua: A Practical Course in Spoken Chinese*; ISBN: 0 9590735 0 7; 1984, 1989, 1992; 101 pp.; softcover: AUS $16.99. [Cassettes available from The Language Centre, University of Sydney NSW 2006, Australia.]

• A. D. Syrokomla-Stefanowska and Mabel Lee, *Basic Chinese Grammar and Sentence Patterns*; ISBN: 0 9590735 1 5; 1986, 1989, 1992; 99 pp.; softcover: AUS $16.99. [Cassettes available from The Language Centre, University of Sydney NSW 2006, Australia.]

• *Readings in Modern Chinese*. Compiled by Liu Wei-ping, Mabel Lee, A. J. Prince, Lily Shaw Lee and R. S. W. Hsu; ISBN: 0 9590735 4 X; 161 pp.; 1988, 1990, 1992; softcover: AUS $30.00. [Cassettes available from The Language Centre, University of Sydney NSW 2006, Australia.]